Madame de (Henriette Elizabeth) Witt

The Lady of Latham

Being the Life and Original Letters of Charlotte de la Tremoille

Madame de (Henriette Elizabeth) Witt

The Lady of Latham
Being the Life and Original Letters of Charlotte de la Tremoille

ISBN/EAN: 9783337137601

Printed in Europe, USA, Canada, Australia, Japan

Cover: Foto ©Raphael Reischuk / pixelio.de

More available books at **www.hansebooks.com**

THE

LADY OF LATHAM;

BEING THE

LIFE AND ORIGINAL LETTERS

OF

CHARLOTTE DE LA TRÉMOILLE,

COUNTESS OF DERBY.

BY

MADAME GUIZOT DE WITT.

WITH A PORTRAIT.

LONDON:

SMITH, ELDER & CO., 15, WATERLOO PLACE.

1869.

CONTENTS.

———◆◆◆———

PREFACE.

———◆◆———

WHY has Sir Walter Scott, that great painter of life and character, so completely failed in his portraiture of the Countess of Derby—the "Lady of Latham" as she is still called in the neighbourhood—who plays such a prominent part in his romance of *Peveril of the Peak?* How is it that, in addition to all the liberties he has taken with historical facts, he has made of this noble lady, as simple as she was heroic, a mere queen of melodrama? It must be because he only knew her by her exploits, and not her personal self at all. Into the depths of her heart he had never penetrated. But, strange to say, we are now enabled to do this.

The veritable and original letters of Charlotte de la Trémoille, Countess of Derby, to her mother,

Charlotte de Nassau, and her sister-in-law, Marie de la Tour d'Auvergne, have lately been discovered, by the descendant of these illustrious women, the present Duc de la Trémoille. The correspondence of ancient families has, in France, necessarily gone through strange vicissitudes : these precious papers were found hidden in a barrel at the bottom of a cellar. They are very numerous, and yellow with age and damp. Many of them are in cypher, but the care of the Duchesse de la Trémoille—to whom most of them were addressed—has, in all cases, added the key: so that they are quite intelligible. The dates would have been difficult to guess at, but that the same sisterly hand has marked them at the back of almost every letter. The whole have been confided to me by M. le Duc de la Trémoille ; and thus I have been enabled to study for my own pleasure, and, by his permission, to make public, the inner life of this remarkable woman,—as unfolded by herself to her dearest and nearest of kin, in this correspondence, which extends over forty years. With it I have interwoven a thread of necessary biography, and of the history of the period ; in which I have largely made use of an old book, the *Genealogical History of the House of Stanley;* also Captain Halsall's relation of the *Siege of Latham House,* and the *State Trials.* And, although the facts of the trial and execution of Lord Derby are sufficiently well known, I have preferred to give them at length—both because the *dénouement* was indispensable to the drama, and because the portrait of the noble husband ought to stand beside that of the heroic wife. The publications of the Cheetham Society have also assisted me much.

With my thanks to my translators, who have so skilfully reproduced in English—and as yet it appears *only* in English—the story of one Frenchwoman told by another; and my acknowledgments to the Earl of Derby for having lent the portrait of his illustrious ancestress to be engraved here;—I entrust to the good-will of the British public these curious remains— discovered two centuries after her death—of one of the most notable women in British history.

GUIZOT DE WITT.

THE LADY OF LATHAM.

CHAPTER I.

PARENTAGE AND EARLY DAYS.

Our lives have not been cast, nor were those of our
fathers, in quiet times, and the future does not offer
the prospect of more repose to our children ; but when
we revert to the history of past centuries we find its
records darkened by so many political convulsions, so
many social revolutions, such sudden and cruel changes
in the fortunes of families, that we turn with something
like relief to the age in which our lot has fallen, and
learn to estimate at its true value the personal security
which we enjoy.   It is well sometimes to look back to
the past, to reflect on its trials and its periods of
violence and suffering, that we may refresh our souls

I

by the example of the virtues displayed in those rude
and cruel times.

Born in the midst of the religious wars of France,
Charlotte de la Trémoille, Countess of Derby, experienced in England all the shocks of the Rebellion of
1640 and of the Protectorate of Cromwell, and died
in 1664, only three years after the restoration of
Charles II. There was, indeed, no calamity that she
had not seen, no sorrow, public or private, that she
had not suffered.

France was hardly beginning to breathe under the
government of Henry IV., when, at the Château of
Thouars,* in 1601, Charlotte was born. Her father,
Claude de la Trémoille, then in his thirty-fifth year, had
been a soldier from his earliest youth, having served
in the royal armies against the Protestants. He afterwards embraced the Reformed religion, and, from his
rank no less than his merit, soon became one of the
foremost men of his party. He sided with the King of
Navarre against the League, fought bravely at Coutras,
was one of the chief Protestants who went to the
succour of Henry III., at that time besieged in Tours
by the Duc de Mayenne, and after their reconciliation
accompanied the two kings to the siege of Paris.

* The Château of Thouars was situated in that part of ancient
Poitou which now forms the department of Deux Sèvres.

Henry III. was assassinated just as the French
Protestants began to look for the triumph of their
faith and the realization of their hopes. After his
death Claude de la Trémoille fought at the side
of Henry IV. at Ivry, and at the siege of Rouen.
Henry's recantation suddenly extinguished the hopes
of Protestantism, and, though its adherents remained
faithful, their ardour was gone.

The King had paid dearly for the submission of
the League, and had few favours left to bestow upon
his faithful companions in arms, who had " carried him
on their shoulders on this side the Loire, and who had
spent in his service their blood and their substance."
M. de Rosny alone was able to maintain his position
at Court—thanks to a friendship which dated from
childhood, as well as to his own able and faithful services. His profoundly politic mind was little fettered
by that severity of conscience which chained M. du
Plessis-Mornay in his government of Saumur, far
removed from the Court and its splendours.

M. de la Trémoille did not concern himself with
politics; the King had need of his sword—and in
1595 he fought so bravely at the battle of Fontaine-
Française that, as a reward, the property of Thouars
was erected into a peerage.

The great Catholic nobles now reappeared at

Court, and there was no longer any room for the
Protestants. Gradually they left Paris, and retired to
their estates and châteaux, seeking and finding some
occupation from time to time in a synod or general
assembly of the deputies of the churches. It was at
Châtellerault, in 1598, on the occasion of one of these
gatherings, that the marriage contract was signed
between Claude de la Trémoille, Duc de Thouars,
Peer of France, Prince of Tarente and of Talmont, and
the most high and puissant Lady Charlotte Brabantine
de Nassau, daughter of William the Silent, Prince of
Orange, and of his third wife, Charlotte de Bourbon
Montpensier.

A great heritage was it, this blood of the glorious
Nassau race ; and the Countess of Derby was destined
to transmit it untarnished.

The times were hard for the Reformers. In vain
was the free exercise of their religion secured to them
by the Edict of Nantes in 1598 : the animosity of the
Court triumphed over the goodwill of the King, and
ominous clouds of a mournful future were already
gathering over their heads. Restless and undis-
ciplined, the deputies of the churches refused to listen
to the wise and loyal counsels of M. du Plessis-
Mornay ; the political tendencies of the party began
to appear ; the Duc de Bouillon, deeply compromised

in the affairs of the Maréchal de Biron, had just quitted France, and the Duc de la Trémoille now never left his Château of Thouars. He had four children, two sons and two daughters, and he lived in great splendour on his estate, where he gave a magnificent reception to M. de Rosny, who had just entered upon the government of Poitou.

The Duc de Bouillon had been forced to relinquish all his towns and châteaux, with the exception of the fortress of Sedan, which belonged to him independently of his sovereign.

M. de Rosny did not conceal from M. de la Trémoille that his brother-in-law was in great danger, and that the King was very much irritated against him.

Henri de la Tour d'Auvergne had owed his marriage with Charlotte de la Marck, heiress of the Bouillons, to the favour of Henry IV. She died, leaving him in possession of all her wealth ; and he took for his second wife Elizabeth of Nassau, daughter of William the Silent and of Louise de Coligny, his fourth wife : she was, consequently, the sister of Madame de la Trémoille, and the King's displeasure against the Duc de Bouillon troubled the peace which the family at Thouars had hitherto enjoyed.

M. de Rosny advised M. de la Trémoille to appear again at Court. "The King intends to continue the war," he said; "and you must serve against Spain."

M. de la Trémoille was still young; for many years he had lived in idleness, annoyed at not being in active service; and he allowed something like a promise to escape him, which promise M. de Rosny, on his return to Court, would not suffer him to forget.

The King was desirous of seeing about him those of his servants who were of the Reformed religion, not thinking it safe to leave them in their châteaux, where they might employ themselves in hatching plots.

M. de la Trémoille had resolved to start for the Court, in spite of his wife's misgivings and those of M. du Plessis, who was on a visit at Thouars.

" I see no reason for your going, except the words which have escaped your lips," said the Governor of Saumur to him.

" But if I could get employment?" said M. de la Trémoille.

M. du Plessis shook his head.

He had scarcely returned to Bonmoy, near Saumur, when he heard from Madame de la Trémoille that her husband had been seized with gout in the arm, and, if he were not speedily better, she begged him to come to them. On the night of the third day she sent him word that, if he wished to see his friend alive, he must come quickly.

Arriving there he found M. de la Trémoille prostrated with fever, and almost constantly insensible. He recovered, however, from this state of torpor, and showed his joy on seeing M. du Plessis again by many expressions, which, though short and broken, displayed all his usual clearness. He was able to commend to this dear friend his wife and children, who were about to lose him so early, and in such troubled times.

But the cares of this present life were beginning to fade from his view. M. du Plessis spoke to him of his hope of salvation.

"No other matter concerns me now," said the dying man; and, disregarding everything else, he so collected his thoughts that, when any one spoke to him of a future life, he always replied with some sentence which showed his readiness to die, the full assurance of his faith in Christ, and the clearheadedness for which he had been so remarkable when in health.*

He was breathing his last when Madame de la Trémoille, who had never left her husband's pillow except to nurse her daughter Charlotte in small-pox,

* *Memoirs of Madame du Plessis-Mornay.*

was told that the Princesse de Condé, sister of the Duc de la Trémoille, wished to see him. She was detained at some distance by an accident to her carriage, and she begged her sister-in-law to send for her.

The Princesse de Condé had been for a long time on bad terms with her brother. Evil reports had been circulated about her at the time of her husband's death. She had been accused of having poisoned him, and had had some trouble to establish the legitimacy of her son, who was born after the death of the Prince. Moreover, since 1596, she had abjured the Reformed faith, and had given up the little Prince de Condé, her son, into the King's hands, that he might be brought up in the Catholic religion.

So many offences could not be atoned for by one tardy visit; nor was there even the hope of a reconciliation, for M. de la Trémoille never spoke again.

"I cannot see her," exclaimed the Duchess. "She will be the death of her brother, and the sight of her would kill me. M. du Plessis, do not suffer her to come."

M. du Plessis hesitated; he did not feel this matter so keenly as the poor wife. Fully expecting his friend's death, he was unwilling to banish the sister from her brother's dying bed, which perhaps might arouse in her some salutary impressions.

But the Duchesse de la Trémoille, ordinarily so

calm, was now beside herself with grief. M. du Plessis was forced to write to the Princesse as respectful a letter as he could, begging her to put off her visit till another time. She continued her journey without going to Thouars ; but she never forgave this affront, which she attributed to M. du Plessis, who had some difficulty in clearing himself with the King on this score.

Just as the Princesse de Condé received the letter of M. du Plessis, her brother died at the Château of Thouars, in his thirty-ninth year, leaving his wife and children to the protection of the Elector Palatine, Prince Maurice of Nassau, the Duc de Bouillon and M. du Plessis, the last of whom was the only one of the three who resided in France, and consequently the only one who could exercise any important influence over the education of the children entrusted to his care. The Duc de la Trémoille had, at his death, desired that his children might be brought up in the Reformed religion.

Great was the sorrow felt, not only at Thouars but throughout the whole Protestant party. The Duc de Bouillon an exile, and the Duc de la Trémoille in his grave,—those of the " Religion," as they were called, had no longer any leaders. M. du Plessis himself, dispirited and out of favour, had not returned

to Court since the fatal conference he had had at
Fontainebleau in 1600 with the Bishop of Evreux,
and every day some slight sign indicated but too
plainly the coldness of the King. M. du Plessis was
reproached for his friendship with M. de la Trémoille,
who was the brother-in-law of the Duc de Bouillon,
still a rebel. Wherefore, it was asked, did M. du
Plessis associate with such malcontents ?

Meanwhile the Reformers were uneasy concerning
the King's supposed sentiments towards them ; more
especially when it was known that his Majesty desired
to have the little Duc de la Trémoille, who, born in
1599, was only five years old at his father's death,
entrusted to him to be educated with the Dauphin.

Madame de la Trémoille was overwhelmed by
this news. She had just lost her second daughter,
Elizabeth ; if the King took her son from her the
child would be estranged from the Protestant faith ;
separated from all his natural connections, he would
no longer belong to his mother ;—better that she
saw him lying in his grave ! M. du Plessis, though
more guarded in speech than the poor mother, was
also much alarmed, and caused it to be represented
to the King that the Reformed party would be justly
suspicious if all the children destined to be their
future leaders were taken away from them ; that they

had already lost the Prince de Condé ; and it concerned his Majesty not to irritate his faithful subjects for the sake of so trifling an advantage as the presence of a child at Court.

The King yielded, and Henri de la Trémoille remained at Thouars during the first year of his mother's widowhood.

In 1605 she went alone to Court, leaving her children at Thouars, as we learn from the letters she received from her daughter Charlotte.

Amongst the important papers of the Trémoille family, side by side with parchments weighted with pompous titles, or long enumerations of estates and seignorial rights, it is touching to see the ruled paper and the large writing which indicate those first letters written by the child who was destined to accomplish such great things.

Charlotte was about five or six years old when she wrote thus to her mother :—

" MADAME,—Since you went away, I have become very good. Thank God, you will find me quite learned. I know seventeen Psalms, all the quatrains of Pibrac, all the huitains of Zamariel, and, above all, I can talk Latin. My little brother is so pretty ! he could not be prettier; when visitors come he is quite

enough to entertain them.   It seems, Madame, a very
long time since we saw you.   Pray love me.   M. de
St. Christophe says you are well, for which I have
thanked God.   I pray to God for you.   I humbly
kiss the hands of my good aunt and of my little
cousins.

  " I am, Madame,

    " Your very humble and very obedient·

    and good daughter,

     " CHARLOTTE DE LA TRÉMOILLE."

Most Protestant families have kept up the pious
habit of learning the Psalms by heart; some people
yet remember the quatrains of Pibrac; but who has
ever heard of the huitains of Zamariel? The
measure of the verse and the name of the poet
have alike vanished from the memory of man.

It would seem that the Duchesse de la Trémoille
was often absent from Thouars while the education
of Charlotte was going on.   Her children sometimes
accompanied her, as we see by a letter of Charlotte's
from Paris, addressed to her brother the little Duc de
la Trémoille ; but they more often remained in the
country while their mother resided at Court or visited
her Dutch relations.   In her absence, however, Madame
de la Trémoille kept up the direction of their education;

and she was evidently well informed of their faults as well as of their progress, for her daughter writes thus to her at the Hague, in 1609 :—

"MADAME,—I am very sorry that I have been disobedient to you, but I hope you will never again have occasion to complain of me. Although I have not been very good, I hope to be so good for the future that you will have no cause of dissatisfaction; and that Madame my grandmamma, and Messieurs my uncles,* will not find me ungrateful any more, but hoping to render them obedient and very humble service. This new year they have shown their kindness by giving me beautiful New Year's presents ; Madame" (the Princess of Orange), "a carcanet of diamonds and rubies ; Monsieur le Prince d'Orange, some earrings ; his Excellency, three dozen of pearl and ruby buttons. Monsieur my uncle has given me a dress of silver tissue. M. Suart has done what you told him. Pray love me always; and I will remain all my life, Madame,

"Your very humble and very obedient
daughter and servant,

"CHARLOTTE DE LA TRÉMOILLE."

* The Princess of Orange, Louise de Coligny, Maurice of Nassau, and Prince Frederic Henry, his brother.

Amongst so many pearls and diamonds let us hope that poor little Charlotte had received from her mother one of those beautiful dolls, in the costume of a Frieslandic lady, with red cheeks, a lace cap, and a gold band on her brow, which must surely have delighted the hearts of little Dutch girls then, as they do still. Later in her life we detect in her a tenderness for dolls, which makes us believe that the associations of her childhood were not exclusively with earring drops and silver-tissue dresses.

Charlotte is again with her mother in 1609, and for ten years the only letters of hers we have are to her brother, the Duc de la Trémoille. Generally separated from his family, he is a very lazy correspondent, sometimes even, to his mother's indignation, employing the pen of a stranger. In 1619 he married his cousin, Marie de la Tour d'Auvergne, daughter of the Duc de Bouillon and of Elizabeth of Nassau ; a union which entirely satisfied his mother, and gave to Charlotte a true sister, whose devotion and affection were to endure as long as her life. From the year 1620 we find her at Thouars, with the young Duchesse de la Trémoille. M. du Plessis, also, came to visit them from his Château de la Forêt sur Sèvres. Though sad and lonely, he had evidently considerable influence, and was of much importance in the family of his friend.

Charlotte was at this time nineteen years of age. She does not appear to have been very robust; she had had fever, and tells her mother that she was taken ill at a great dinner. Throughout her life, indeed, her mind was stronger than her body, and her letters often contain accounts of attacks of illness. Her correspondence with her mother, however, is not the less active on that account. She seizes every opportunity of sending her news of their country doings, of the comings and goings, the questions and the answers of M. du Plessis. But her writing, so legible on the ruled paper and under the eye of " *sa mie*," degenerates sadly. She has no longer time to trouble herself about orthography; she writes in such defiance of rules and principles that it is often necessary to read the sentences aloud to gather her meaning. Madame la Duchesse de la Trémoille, who used to compliment her on her writing, has no longer any cause for approbation. The silver-tissue dresses, and even the gold fringe, have again become prominent features in the details of her life. The numerous accounts preserved by the Duc de la Trémoille's steward testify to her large expenditure and very decided taste for dress ; Mademoiselle's jeweller and tailor fill an important place in the family budget. One would like to believe in the truth of a portrait of Charlotte, painted by Rubens at the time of her marriage. It represents her in good health, bright and blooming. She wears a corsage of scarlet satin, and a hat with white feathers, and is looking over her shoulder, and smiling with an arch expression.

Indications of liveliness and animation appear in her letters even through the antiquated formalities of the period, and the profound respect with which her mother inspired her. " I will not repeat the news of this place," she writes to her mother; " M. du Plessis will tell it so much better than I can write it. The subject most spoken of just now is the building of a church." And, after having consulted her mother to know if she ought to contribute to the undertaking, she adds: " My brother has not shown us the letter you wrote him, and he has not shown that or any other to my sister-in-law, although she shows him all hers. She often tells me that he does not take pains to be in as good temper as when you were here; and that she saw you were of the greatest use to him. It seems to me, however, that they get on very well together; although he is often so dull that one cannot coax a word out of him. With me he is always on the best possible terms, and often comes to look for me in my room."

The intimacy between the brother and sister was not to last; but the confidence between the sisters-in-law was destined to go on increasing, in spite of a separation of nearly forty years, and to end only with life.

CHAPTER II.

MARRIAGE AND FIRST YEARS IN ENGLAND.

CHARLOTTE must have been again with her mother, who had taken her to Paris, when she writes to her sister-in-law, Madame de la Trémoille: "You will have learned from others how well the arrangement of our fortunes has turned. out, thank God! and how well Madame has treated my brother; how much better than he could have ventured to hope. For my part I am not surprised, when I think of her invariable goodness. What she reserves is less for her own benefit, than for that of others."

"Madame," as her children always called her, doubtless made her family arrangements with the view of entering on some treaty of marriage for her daughter, for at the beginning of 1626, we find them at the Hague, at the Court of Prince Frederic Henry of Nassau, her uncle, the brother of Prince

Maurice, who had died the preceding year. The only letter of this period that we possess is addressed by Charlotte to her sister-in-law. According to the custom of the time, she makes no allusion in it to her coming marriage with Lord Strange. The negotiations for this alliance were nevertheless far advanced, as we may gather from the correspondence of the lawyers with the Duchess Dowager.

But Charlotte is out of spirits and not happy in Holland. "We are in a country where there is very little zeal," she writes ; "and it is entirely without reason that they are suspected of it : as for going to war in defence of religion, that is far from their thoughts. . . . The French must not look for aid in this country. Your brother, who governs things here as well as he can, is not amongst those who are most content. Indeed, scarcely anybody is content ; here as elsewhere all the world complains of its leaders. In fact, I see that the world is a place in which it is very difficult to live ; the longer I am in it the more clearly I perceive this. May it please God to give me His guidance in it, and you, my heart! perfect content."

Can it be the near prospect of her marriage, or only the *ennui* of her life at the Hague, that suggests to Charlotte de la Trémoille these serious reflections ?

She mingles with them a description of a ballet danced
at Court before the Persian Ambassador :

" He believes that women who dance are good
for nothing," she writes; "but he has been made to
change this opinion. He has a good understanding,
and is very polite. He thinks that his Excellency
is Emperor of this country, and cannot be persuaded
that the States are above him."

A genuine daughter of the house of Nassau,
Charlotte de la Trémoille nourished a little bitterness
against the States, and thought this opinion of the
Ambassador very wise and sensible.

The struggle had already begun which was to
terminate in the ruin of the Republican party and the
bloody death of the brothers De Witt.

At the Hague, in July, 1626, Charlotte de la
Trémoille was married to James Stanley, Lord Strange,
son of the Earl of Derby (or " d'Herbie," as it was
written in France), and Elizabeth de Vere, daughter of
the Earl of Oxford. He was only twenty years old,—
handsome, brave, and cultivated, and descended from
a family in itself one of the most illustrious in England,
and which had also intermarried with the blood royal.
He possessed considerable influence in the counties
of Chester and Lancaster, and was heir to the Lordship of the Isle of Man. Charlotte's great grief on

her marriage was her separation from all whom she loved at a time when sea voyages were difficult, often even dangerous, when letters were always long on the road, and were not unfrequently lost.   She was destined never to return to France, and, though to the last day of her life cherishing the hope of a re-union, she never again beheld that sister who was so dear—who remained to her so steadfastly faithful.

In conformity with the custom of her day, the Duchesse de la Trémoille accompanied her daughter to England to establish her in her new home.   It was the month of August, 1626, more than a year after the accession of Charles I. to the throne of England, and rather less than a year after his marriage with Henrietta Maria, sister of Louis XIII., and daughter of Henry IV. and Marie de Medicis,— a Princess at once charming and frivolous, capricious and witty, with whom he was passionately in love.

Charles had scarcely begun his reign when serious disagreements arose between him and his people. The great political movement which had gradually changed all the monarchies of Europe into absolute sovereignties had begun to make itself felt in England also.   No monarch had adopted the principles of absolutism with greater eagerness than the vain and feeble James I.   He had brought up his son

in the doctrines that he himself held, and in that
romantic visit which Charles had made to Spain to
secure the heart as well as the hand of the Infanta,
the Prince had seen royalty under its most majestic
and sovereign aspect, rarely opposed, and always
certain in the end to rise above all opposition by
the force of its own will, obtaining from its followers
and the people a respect and devotion almost religious.
" Charles's marriage with the Infanta did not take place,
but Spanish royalty remained in his imagination
the idealization of the regal condition, being in perfect
harmony with the natural gravity of his own character,
and with a certain dignity, heightened by a little
timidity, which made him dread the efforts and the
struggles of a liberal Government."*

This liberal Government, to which neither kings
nor people on the continent ever gave a thought,
possessed in England an element unknown elsewhere.
The old aristocracy were subdued as in France,
but a great middle class composed of country gentlemen and bourgeois had formed itself there earlier
than in other countries, and was rapidly developing.
The Reformation had given a great stimulus to the
up-growth of this class ; the English people, called
on to decide for themselves in matters which con-

* Guizot's *History of the English Revolution.*

cerned their eternal welfare, assumed the right of judgment in political matters ; and it was in vain that Charles, by convoking the Parliament, a few months after his accession to the throne, hoped to strengthen the bonds which united him to his people : "disunion was in reality complete, for both the one and the other thought as sovereigns." *

The dissensions between the King and the people grew more and more serious, and the dissolution of the Parliament was not long in coming. For six months the King had tried to govern alone, but his growing embarrassments had obliged him to reassemble his Parliament. They had lately pretended to redress the public grievances. Now they accused the Duke of Buckingham, and demanded his banishment. He was the friend and counsellor of the King, as he had been of his father; all the faults of the Royal Government were attributed to him, and the accusations with which the public voice had charged him were now brought against him by the Commons. The Duke refuted them, and for the most part with success. But it was his favour and influence with the King that was the point aimed at by the Parliament.

In the month of August, 1626, the young Lady Strange arrived in England, and, it is said, she was

* GUIZOT's *History of the English Revolution.*

for a short time in London in attendance on the
Queen Henrietta Maria; but of this I find no evidence
in her correspondence.

In August, 1627, we find her at Latham House,
the mansion of her husband in the county of Lancaster,
whence she announces to her mother her anticipation
of her first-born, adding :—" The time of our stay
here is not yet determined, but if the twenty thousand
crowns do not come it will be a hard matter to get
away. Your son-in-law is quite well, thank God, and
often goes out hunting. On Monday we are to have
a great many people here, for it is our wedding-day,
and my husband is going from home for several days
with a number of gentlemen. He shows me the
utmost affection, and God gives us grace to live in
much happiness and peace of mind. We are in
trouble about the Isle of Man, and if Chateauneuf
had been here we should have offered him the charge
of it. The appointment is worth a thousand francs,
and in a place where one can live almost for nothing."

The twenty thousand crowns which Lady Strange
expected did not come, and the family remained at
Latham. The Earl of Derby had relinquished this
house to his son, and he himself lived at Chester,
where his daughter-in-law paid him a visit, as she
writes to her mother towards the end of the year

1627.   All her late letters had been lost, as was often the case; and she recapitulates the little events of her life.

"I wrote you word, Madame, that I had seen my father-in-law at Chester, where he always lives, never desiring to go to any of his other houses; he has been there now for three or four years.   He spoke to me in French, and said very kind things to me, calling me lady and mistress of the house, a position which he said he wished no other woman to hold; that I had the law in my own hands entirely.   We were very well received in the town; though we were not expected many people came to meet us.   I told you also, Madame, how much I liked Latham House, and that I had every reason to thank God and you for having married me so happily.   I do not doubt, Madame, that you will do everything in your power with regard to my money; indeed I expect this from you, and certes, Madame, necessity constrains me to importune you in the matter more than I ought; your goodness emboldens me to do so, and truly, my happiness partly depends on it, that I may be able to shut the mouths of some people who do not love foreigners, though, thank God, the best of these wish me no harm.   I am thankful to say that your son is now quite well, having had no return of his complaint.

He is constantly out of doors, the air being very good
for him."

Lord Strange must, however, have come in before
his wife's letter was despatched, for the postscript is
in his handwriting. Both handwriting and spelling
are much better than Charlotte's.

" MADAME,—I cannot allow my wife to write without
myself thanking you for the honour you have done
me; if I could write with as much ease in your
language as in my own, I would not fail to assure you
on all occasions that I shall always be, Madame, your
very humble and very obedient son and servant,

" J. STRANGE."

The money difficulties which continued to weigh
upon Charlotte all through her life were already
beginning to trouble her. Her own family was
illustrious, powerful, and possessed of great estates,
but the late wars had burdened these estates with
many debts. Towns and castles belonging to the
Duc de la Trémoille had been seized by the League;
amongst others the fortress of Rochefort, which
M. du Plessis and the Maréchal d'Aumont had
in vain attempted to recover. The farmers paid
their rents irregularly, and the estates could not be

sold; consequently the Duc de la Trémoille was unable to send his sister's fortune to England.

The historian of the house of Stanley asserts that she received fifty thousand pounds sterling; but, even if so large a sum had been due to her by her brother after their mother's death, and when the heritage of their brother the Count of Laval fell in, I doubt if the house of Derby ever derived such great benefit from it.

The embarrassments of the family with which Charlotte had allied herself were also very great. Lord Derby, the father of Lord Strange, had succeeded his brother in the title; but a considerable portion of the estates was not entailed upon heirs male, but constituted dowries for the three daughters of Ferdinand, the fifth Earl. The division was settled only after numerous and expensive lawsuits; the possession of the Isle of Man especially being the subject of long disputes, which were at last terminated by an Act of Parliament.

William, sixth Earl of Derby, found himself obliged to support all the honour and magnificence of the House of Stanley with a fortune greatly inferior to that of his ancestors. His estates were burdened with debts, and Charlotte's fortune was necessary to clear them.

Since the month of November, 1626, she had
received only one sum of twelve hundred pounds
sterling, for which we find a receipt. She writes
again towards the end of 1627 :—

"I am not without anxiety about many things;
but God of His goodness will provide for all. I
forgot to tell you, Madame, that my husband is on
the point of doing that which he is bound in honour
to do, though I have never said a word to him about
it ; and he has even fixed the sum at two thousand
pounds sterling" (her jointure). "Although I hope,
please God, that I may never need it, yet I shall
always feel deep obligation to him. I owe it entirely
to his goodness, which makes me still more anxious
that he should derive some benefit from my fortune,
from which he has as yet received so little help. I
am sure, Madame, that your goodness will see, even
better than I do, what need we have of it, and also
how happy it would make me to afford some relief to
this house, upon which I have hitherto brought
nothing but expense."

But it was in vain for Lady Strange to write, or
for her mother to speak : the payment, not only of
the capital, but even the interest, of her fortune was
delayed ; and this was a constant grief to her.

"I should be very glad now to have it known

that my fortune was not only a thing talked of, but a fact," she writes.   " This makes me very unhappy."

The civil war was now raging in France in all its horrors. Louis XIII. and Richelieu were besieging La Rochelle, while the Duc de Rohan, at the head of the Protestant army, occupied the country in the southern provinces. His mother, the Duchess Dowager, was shut up in the fortress, within her own house, which, however, she had no wish to leave.   " Do not be uneasy about me," she wrote to her son ; and both by her words and her example she kept up the courage of the citizens of La Rochelle.

In England, much concern was felt for the dangerous position of the French Protestants ; and the Duke of Buckingham resolved to turn this generous sympathy to the profit of his passions and his personal interests. He was in love with Queen Anne of Austria, and being kept at a distance from the French Court by the vigilance of Richelieu, he induced the King his master to declare war against France, proposing that he should himself take command of the fleet which was to attempt the deliverance of La Rochelle. Very little money could be obtained by means of a forced loan to fit out the expedition. The English people distrusted the sincerity of Buckingham's zeal ; they might no less have doubted his ability.

On the 29th of October, 1627, the expedition
which he led was stranded before La Rochelle, and
this misfortune was universally attributed to the
incapacity of the leader. Lady Strange expresses
the feeling of the Court rather than that of the
country when she writes to her mother on the
29th of November :

"Here nothing is spoken of but the misfortune
which has happened to the Duke. He is not blamed
for it, but the fault is laid on the delay of the
intended succours." And she adds : " He has
brought back with him M. de Soubise " (brother of
the Duc de Rohan); " I am surprised that he was
willing to return. They say that the former is to
go out again soon with fresh forces. All this makes
me despair of peace. If it were in my power to
make any overtures in this direction, which it is
not, my distance from Court would prevent my
doing so. And, besides, the person who is allied
to us takes no part in politics; not so much that
he has no taste for them, but he is of a certain
disposition unfitted for public life; and, also, he is
not liked by the superior powers." (Does she
speak here of her husband, of her father-in-law,
or of M. de Soubise?) " Besides, his power is not
what it once was, and I think it is diminishing.

I believe also that peace will only come through those who have begun the war. As for the Queen she interferes with nothing, and thinks only of how to kill time. The King and she live very happily together."

Lady Strange was scarcely older than the Queen Henrietta Maria, but she had other things to think of, than of "how to kill time." In the midst of her anxiety for the public welfare, and her desire to see peace re-established between France and England (she seems to have troubled herself very little about the fate of the Protestants of La Rochelle), there re-appear continually her natural human interests in the character of wife and mother. Alone, and far away from her own people, she was expecting her hour of trial. She had hoped for the presence of her mother, but in December, 1627, she thus writes to her sister-in-law :—

"I feel very much as you do, my heart, about Madame's coming to me ; though I longed passion-ately for it, yet the troubles and dangers which I know she must have encountered made me always dread what has happened. But I trust that God will not forsake me, though I am alone, and do not know much about such matters. May it please Him to give me the same happiness as Madame

de Duras :—but, oh! my heart, I must not think
about it any more; I commit myself to God. I
know well, my dear, that you remember me in your
prayers, and that you rejoice with me in my hopes of
motherhood. You may be sure, dear sister, that the
child which God may be pleased to give me will be
devoted to you."

We have no letter from Lady Strange herself
informing her mother of her son's birth ; but on the
26th of January, 1628, Lord Strange writes to the
Duchess :—

" MADAME — Although we had resolved to send
to you by express if possible, yet I have thought
it my duty to inform you by letter of my wife's
safe delivery of a son. I fear that if you should
hear of it from others you might be anxious about
her, whereas she is doing well, and the child also,
thank God. I must leave it to Mademoiselle de
Beaulieu " (a midwife who had come from France)
"to tell you all the particulars. I will only add
that we believe her to be now out of danger,
this being her seventh day, and that she will very
soon write to you herself. Our joy would have
been complete if we could have had the honour
of your presence ; but that will be when God pleases.

That He may long preserve you is the earnest
desire, Madame, of

"Your very humble and

very obedient son and servant,

"STRANGE.

"Madame, I have not written to your sons about
the birth of your grandchild, feeling sure that you
would do us the honour of acquainting them with it."

A month later, Lady Strange writes to her sister-
in-law, informing her of her confinement : " I forgot
to tell you that he is dark," she says, speaking of her
child. " I wish you could see the manner in which
they swaddle infants in this country, for it is lament-
able. Three days after mine was born, he was found
in the middle of the night sucking his thumb.
Imagine the rest ! My husband would have written
to you ; but he does not like to venture in a foreign
language. He is, nevertheless, your humble servant."
And again, on the 17th of April : " I have written to
Madame an account of the baptism of your nephew,
who, by the grace of God, was received into the
Church on Sunday the 30th of March "* (old style).
" He was carried by my sister-in-law, and his train

* The Gregorian calendar had not yet been adopted in England ;
thus we must always reckon ten days forward in these dates.

was borne by four ladies, the wives of knights of this county. I had him dressed in white, after the French fashion; for here they dress children in colours, which I do not like. The Archbishop of Chester baptized him in the Chapel of the Castle, and the only name which he received was that of the King, which you know well. Afterwards, there was a collation; and, both on that day and for several days before and after, the dishes at supper were carried by gentlemen of the county. The King has given him two gilt cups, the usual gift with which he gratifies those on whom he confers the favour of giving his name; but to show us special honour, he has sent me a very pretty present, which is worth quite two thousand crowns: the diamonds are very beautiful, and are all cut with facets. I did not expect this. The Duchess of Richmond (the godmother) gave him a large basin, and a silver-gilt knife, which is used when the loaves of bread have been removed from the table; and to me she gave a turquoise bracelet."

The young father (he was scarcely twenty-two) had the year before been called to the Upper House by the title of Baron Strange, in consequence of an error in the letters of convocation; it having been forgotten that the Barony of Strange was one of the titles that had fallen into abeyance at the death of

Ferdinand, fifth Earl of Derby. This error led to the creation of a new peerage, which reverted in course of time to the House of Athol ; and Lord Strange sat for several years in the House of Lords at the same time as his father, the Earl of Derby.

Early in 1628 the King called a new Parliament. " I write this in much trouble," said Lady Strange, on the 19th of May, " for I fear that my husband must go the day after to-morrow to London. This change is doubly vexatious to me, for the air does not agree with him ; but I hope God will preserve him. Our little one is very well, thank God. I have already, in two of my letters, begged you to send me some long frocks, and now I must ask you the same thing again, for he is very strong, thank God, for his age ; and in this country, where they put into robes infants of a month or six weeks old, I am thought out of my senses because I have not yet given him any. I also begged you for some child's caps. I hope these will all come together. It will be an amusement for me in the absence of my boy's father, which I dread greatly, for I have never been so far from him before ; and in these times there is always something to fear. God grant that all that is resolved upon in this Parliament may be for His glory, and for the good of the King and the country. Here nothing is talked of but the victories of M. de Rohan. I wish I knew the truth about them."

Lord Strange did not go to London. "My husband was advised not to go to the Parliament," wrote his wife in the month of June, 1628. "Things are in great confusion there. One day everything is broken off, on the next all goes smoothly again. God grant that all may end well."

Things were, indeed, "in great confusion," for the two Houses had just passed, and, after a stormy meeting, had forced the King to give his assent to, the Bill known under the name of the Petition of Rights, an Act establishing anew, and recapitulating in detail, all the liberties and securities acquired by the English people ; immediately after which Charles prorogued the Parliament, on the 26th of June, 1628. Two months later (23rd of August) the Duke of Buckingham was assassinated.

" I am sure, my heart," writes Lady Strange to her sister-in-law, on the 21st of September. " that, before you receive this, you will have heard of the death of the Duke of Buckingham, who was killed by Felton, the lieutenant of a company, to whom he had refused promotion. Felton might very well have made his escape ; but a desire to die, and a gloomy disposition, seem to have led him to commit the act. The

Duke's* wife is very much to be pitied. He loved her devotedly; and she is very good, and the gentlest of women. The King also appeared greatly distressed by the occurrence, and was a whole day without seeing anybody, and without eating till ten o'clock at night. He heard the news at morning prayers; but he did not rise from his devotions. The next day, Sunday, he attended divine service, and sent word to the Duchess that he would be as a husband to her, a father to her children, and a master to her servants. You may judge what a great change this will make at Court. God grant that it may be for His glory, and may lead to a happy peace."

Meantime, the subsidies voted by Parliament were levied. "To these subsidies the highest people contribute, each according to his means," Lady Strange writes to her mother. "My husband's great grandfather, whose income was certainly three times as large as ours, was taxed at four thousand francs, and yet we have to give as much as he did. This arrangement is very disadvantageous for the nobility; but the people are relieved by it, and the King has no power to levy these subsidies except when they are granted by the Parliament, This is not done every year, but only on extraordinary occasions."

* Lady Catherine Manners, daughter of Lord Rutland.

She takes advantage of this opening to press once more for the payment of her marriage portion.

"If Chateauneuf has the honour of seeing you, he can tell you, Madame, how much I and my house suffer from not having had this sum of twenty thousand crowns. If I had not so good a husband, this would perhaps arouse suspicions in him, which, however, thank God, it has not done. What troubles me most is that, by entering this family, I see I have only increased its debts and expenses. Several of my husband's friends became security for the money which he borrowed at the time of his voyage" (to Holland, on the occasion of his marriage), "and this he has never yet been able to repay, which is a great grief to him and to me also, for there is nothing which he hates so much as breaking his word."

But all her anxiety about her fortune and her concern for the public welfare were suddenly swept from Lady Strange's mind by a heavy sorrow which now came upon her, and on her mother and sister-in-law. The Duc de la Trémoille set out for La Rochelle, not to join the Protestants who were defending it, but to take his place in the army of the King, Louis XIII. He was received into the Catholic Church by Cardinal Richelieu, and was immediately afterwards appointed Commander of the Light Cavalry of France.

" I was not altogether unprepared for my brother's change of religion," Lady Strange writes to her mother : " it is a long time since I first heard a report of it ; and, indeed, it was told as a certain fact to the Queen, who, seeing that you, Madame, were counted among the converts, said that she did not believe a word of it.   This, however, made me doubt about my brother.   God has been pleased to send this affliction to you, Madame, and to his family.   I feel my part of it keenly ; more indeed, than I could have believed. The letter which you were so good as to send me from him certainly shows that he has suffered ; but I cannot believe what he says, that worldly motives had not more to do with it than anything else ; the Catholics, at any rate, speak of it thus."   And in writing to her sister-in-law, who had just given birth to a little girl, she says :—" I love and honour you with all my heart ; and this makes me feel doubly your husband's change of religion, which has been a great blow to me.   I can hardly believe it ; but I trust that God will change his heart.   Certainly, few people, in times like these, could believe that he has not been led to do it from worldly considerations.   In truth, if one were to think only of these, no one would remain long of our religion.   I feel much for the pain it will cost you not to follow the stream ; nevertheless,

my heart, I doubt not that you will be able to resist.
God will give you strength greater than your own,
and we shall see you doing double service for His
glory, inasmuch as you must henceforth stand alone."

Lady Strange had other reasons to be displeased
with the Duc de la Trémoille, for she writes to her
mother :—" I have been told that if my brother had
had the power, he would have possessed himself of
my fortune but that the laws of the country do not
permit it. He began by changing towards me. I must
confess, Madame, that but for my respect for you, I
do not know to what lengths I might not be driven in
consequence of the ill-feeling which he has shown for
us." She concludes by entreating her mother's pardon
for her brother, the Count de Laval, who had been for
several years living as a refugee in Holland, in consequence of vicious follies which he had committed in
France.

While the ladies of the house of Trémoille were
mourning over the fall of its head, the English Parliament met again (January 20, 1629), and this time
Lord Strange thought it his duty to be present. He
took with him to London his wife, who was again
pregnant, and his son. Three months had not passed
before dissensions more bitter than ever arose between
the King and his Commons. Parliament was once

more dissolved; and Charles boldly announced his intention of governing alone for the future.

Lord Strange was still in London when his wife gave birth to a little girl, who died soon after, having been smothered in its nurse's bed. "This affects and grieves me so extremely, that without God's help I do not know what I should do," writes Lady Strange to her sister-in-law. But the child was a mere infant, her little boy was well, and the mother seems to have consoled herself very quickly. She returned to Latham towards the end of the year 1629, and we meet with no more letters from her till October 1631. She writes then in the deepest grief for the death of her mother, which took place at the Château Renard, in the month of August.

"DEAR SISTER,—It has been a comfort to me in my great affliction to receive the honour of your letters, and above all to know that I retain your friendship, which is one of the things that I desire most in this world. I trust that you will always preserve your affection for me, not that I deserve it, but for the sake of her whom we both deplore, seeing that you do not doubt of hers for me, and that I have always loved you next to herself. Now that God has taken her from us I put you in her place and pay you all the

respect, duty, and love, that I felt for her. . . . . God
has taken her away to punish us and to make her
happy. I never liked the Château Renard; she was
so far from all her children, and had no sort of
amusement near her; but God intended by this
means to wean her from the world. For myself I
confess that I no longer find any pleasure here. . . . .
You desire me to tell you of my brother the Count
de Laval's sorrow : I did not see him till three
days after this news reached us : I saw him shed
a few tears, but very soon afterwards he was as
gay as ever. I must confess, that if I were in his
place I should never be happy again. I cannot tell
whether he tries to deceive himself; but at least he
expresses no sorrow for the past. He only sees me
occasionally, and he shows an impatience in my
presence and a desire to escape out of the house.
I hear such different accounts of him that I do not
know what to believe."

This was written from Chelsea, where Lady
Strange had been living for some months. She
there gave birth to a little girl, who received the
name of Henrietta Maria at her baptism; probably
the Queen was her godmother, the little Charles not
being able to receive that honour because his god-

father had been the King. About the same time a second daughter, named Marie Charlotte, was born to the Duchesse de la Trémoille.

Six months passed during which no letters have been preserved; but in March, 1632, we find Lady Strange again in London, on her way to the Hague, probably to arrange the affairs of Charlotte of Nassau.

Some differences had lately arisen between the Duc de la Trémoille and the Count de Laval, which caused their sister much distress.

"I hope your husband will comply with the last wish of her who brought us all into the world," she writes. "For your part, dear sister, I doubt not that your goodness and generosity will surmount all other considerations."

The generosity and indulgence of the Duchesse de la Trémoille were more than once to be put to the test by the Count de Laval. He had had several children by an Englishwoman, Miss Orpe. In 1634 this person, being in London, set up a claim to be his wife, and assumed the name of Countess de Laval, a proceeding which greatly disturbed Lady Strange, who wrote on the subject to her sister-in-law.

But her chief trouble still continued to be the money from France, which either did not come at all, or reached her only after it had been diminished by exchange. The rents due at Christmas were still unpaid at Midsummer.

"Forgive me, dear sister," she writes on the 20th of October, 1638, "for speaking to you so frankly, but I do it because I know you to be too reasonable and just to consent to anything which is neither. I have no doubt that your son has by this time arrived in Holland" (he had passed through London, but his aunt had not seen him). "He will not find things there so prosperous as usual; God grant that he may have found the Prince of Orange in good health."

Here the correspondence breaks off: from 1638 to 1646, we have only one letter, written in 1640, on the occasion of the death of Mademoiselle de la Trémoille. Letters in these times were often lost on the road; and those which have been preserved in French families have passed through many vicissitudes. Yet this was the most important period of the life of Charlotte de la Trémoille; although in the whole correspondence, stretching over so long a time and continuing for fifteen years beyond this date, not one single allusion is made to those events which have rendered her name illustrious. She seems simply to have done what she believed to be her duty, without seeing anything extraordinary in it, and, after the work was once accomplished, her thoughts appear never to have gone back to the past. Happily her story is here taken up by history, and the documents of the time enable us to make up for the silence of Lady Strange, who was now soon to become Countess of Derby.

CHAPTER III.

THE BEGINNING OF TROUBLES.

SINCE the year 1637, the old Earl of Derby, weary of life, had resolved to relieve himself of the cares attendant on the management of his property; and had resigned everything into the hands of his son, Lord Strange, only reserving for himself a pension of one thousand pounds sterling, to enable him to live in comfort at a country - house which he had purchased on the banks of the Dee, near Chester. In 1640, Lord Strange was associated with his father as Lord Chamberlain of Chester, and in 1642, on his father's death, he succeeded to the title, and Charlotte de la Trémoille, " Madame Strange," as she was called by her relations in France and Holland, took the name which she has made famous—that of Countess of Derby.

Till within a short time of his father's death

Lord Strange had continued to live on his estates, far from the Parliament, and the contests that were being carried on there. Taking no part in politics, though faithfully attached to the King and the ancient constitution of England, he spent his time in intercourse with his friends, in hunting, and in maintaining by turns, in his different houses in the counties of Lancaster and Chester, a princely hospitality, surrounded by his hereditary retainers,— by this means preparing, almost unconsciously, the assistance which he was soon to bring to the King. He had never solicited for himself or for any of his relations either place or favour; nor had he ever profited either by his own connection with the royal family (he was descended from the Duchess of Suffolk, sister of Henry VIII., who had been at one time Queen of France), or by the family ties which the marriage of Lady Derby's cousin, the Prince of Orange, with the Princess Henrietta Maria, had established between that Princess and the Countess. He wished for no higher position than that of an English nobleman, living on his estates, apart from the Court and its favours. But when the Court had no longer any favours to bestow, he left his retirement, and was one of the first who joined the King at York, where Charles

then was, making preparations for the war which
had now become inevitable. He brought to the
royal cause the support of his name and his arms,
and was ready to devote to it both the last drop
of his blood and the last farthing in his purse. A
noble aim and end,—to which alas! his devotion did
indeed attain.

Up to this time, 1642, negotiations were still
being carried on between the King and the Parliament, but the breach between them was becoming
wider every day. Many members of both Houses
had joined Charles at York, and great numbers of
noblemen and country gentlemen had offered him
their services. But, notwithstanding the enthusiasm
which the cause and person of the King were beginning to inspire, the Parliamentary Commissioners
found that there was a growing division amongst
the Royalists; for when it was proposed that a royal
guard should be levied from among the gentlemen
of the neighbourhood, more than fifty, at the head
of whom was Sir Thomas Fairfax, refused to give
in their names; and at a meeting of freeholders,
summoned by the King himself, a petition was
circulated beseeching him to banish all thought of
war, and to be reconciled with his Parliament, and
a copy of this Sir Thomas Fairfax contrived to

place on the pommel of the King's saddle, at the risk of being trampled under his horse's feet.

Neither money, arms, nor even provisions were to be found at York; and, while the loan voted by Parliament was carried by acclamation, the King's Commissioners had the greatest difficulty in collecting from house to house a few trifling contributions, which scarcely sufficed for the support of the royal household. No actual preparations for war had been begun, but the overstrained cord was nearly broken.

The proposals of accommodation sent by the Parliament arrived at York on June 17, 1642, and at once dissipated all hopes of peace. The Houses demanded the complete abolition of the royal prerogative, and claimed for themselves the sole exercise of power. On reading these propositions the King could not restrain his anger.

"If we were to grant what you demand," he said, "we should remain but the image, the sign, the empty phantom of a king,"—and he broke off the negotiations.

The Parliament had been prepared for this termination, and as soon as they received intelligence of it the question of civil war was put to the vote. Only forty-five members voted against it in the House of Commons; and in the House of Lords the Earl of

Portland alone protested. The formation of an army was therefore decreed, and the Earl of Essex was appointed Commander-in-Chief.

The King, on his side, assembled his faithful subjects about him, and in the foremost ranks of his growing army we find Lord Strange, who had already raised among his own dependants a body of three thousand men, well supplied with arms and provisions ; but on finding that the King was destitute of everything at York, and unable to procure arms, he gave up to him at once the whole contents of his arsenals, receiving a promise that he should be supplied afresh from Newcastle, where a magazine had begun to be formed. But this order was never executed ; neither did Lord Strange ever receive the sum of money which the King afterwards allowed him as payment for the arms which he had given up.

" I shall only say," writes this faithful servant of the Crown, " that this might show the King my good intention in the discharge of a good conscience and the preservation of my honour, in spite of envy and malice."*

Envy and malice had, in fact, begun to take alarm at the arrival at Court of a young man who was so

* SEACOME'S *Historical and Genealogical Account of the House of Stanley.*

powerful in his county that the people used to say, " Long live the King and the Earl of Derby!"

He was always surrounded by friends and servants, ready to follow him to the field of battle; but " whether this was more to continue a custom," says the historian of the house of Stanley, " or for the love of his name or person, was hard to say."

The King had resolved to set up his standard, and for the encouragement of his partisans, both nobles and people, had already passed in person through several counties, everywhere earnestly recommending prudence as well as zeal, and proclaiming boldly his attachment to the religion and laws of his country. By two unsuccessful attempts upon Hull and Coventry he had given the Parliamentarians occasion to charge him as the aggressor. But the two parties still hesitated, and, while awaiting the final decision, a meeting was held to fix upon the most convenient place in which to set up the royal standard. At this meeting Lord Strange was present, and, after listening to the arguments put forward in favour of Nottingham, Chester, York, Shrewsbury, and Oxford, he spoke " with a calm and quiet humility," says his biographer. He hoped that the King would take into consideration the claims of the county of Lancaster, urging that it lay as the centre of those counties which

were favourably disposed to the royal cause; that
the people were usually very hardy, and made good
soldiers; that they were all loyally disposed; that he
himself, though the unworthiest of his lieutenants,
would, to the utmost of his estate, contribute to his
service; that he durst promise 3,000 foot and 500
horse, and that he made no doubt but in three days
he could enlist 7,000 men more, thus furnishing to his
Majesty, in the county of Lancaster alone, an army of
10,000 men, to which the accesses from neighbouring
counties might in a short time arise to a considerable
army; and he hoped his Majesty would be able to
march to London walls, before the rebels there could
form an army to oppose him.*

The personal influence of Lord Strange was
evidently very great—so long as he was present. To
the dissatisfaction of the Court party, who were
opposed to him, the King resolved to set up his
standard at Warrington, in the county of Lancaster,
and commissioned Lord Strange to proceed thither and
prepare the people for his reception. He set out, therefore, doubtless seeing Lady Strange at Knowsley by
the way, and, immediately on his return to Lancashire,
he mustered his friends and the King's adherents in
three places, on the heaths by Bury, at Ormskirk,

* SEACOME'S *House of Stanley.*

and at Preston,—to the number of at least sixty thousand men, all well armed.

Having thus seen his hopes crowned with success, Lord Strange intended to have repeated his efforts in Cheshire and in North Wales, where he was lieutenant; but in his absence his enemies had regained their influence over the King, and had urged many reasons against entrusting him with power. It was insinuated that the house of Derby was very powerful in two or three counties; that the old earl was near his end; that Lord Strange was ambitious, and no favourer of the Court, but rather a malcontent; that these levies of troops, about which so much noise was made, were intended to conceal his ambitious designs, for he knew too well his near alliance to the Crown; that those of his name had not always been faithful to the side which they seemed to favour, as witness Lord Stanley, his ancestor, who, though he fought with Richard III. at Bosworth, giving him his son as a hostage, yet turned the battle against him, and crowned, on the field, his own son-in-law, the Earl of Richmond. It was known also that his uncle Ferdinand had boldly declared his pretensions to the throne, and that he himself had married a French lady, a Huguenot, brought up in the pernicious principles of the Low Countries,—of that house of

Nassau which had headed the revolt of the United
Provinces. All these things were dangerous and of
evil example ; it was not safe for his Majesty to trust
himself in such hands.*

Such arguments as these roused the King's
suspicions, and, suddenly changing his plans, he
announced his intention of erecting the royal standard
at Nottingham ; he hastily divested Lord Strange of
the lieutenancy of Chester and North Wales, and
associated with him in that of Lancaster, Lord Rivers,
who had recently been made an earl.

This news reached Lord Strange in the midst of
his preparations for the King's reception, and gave
him some trouble and anxiety of mind, says his
biographer. " Yet, agreeable to his great temper,
he quickly recovered himself, and replied to the
messenger :—

" ' Let my master be happy, though I be miserable,
and if they consult well for him, I shall not be much
concerned what becomes of me. My wife, my family,
and country are very dear to me ; but if my prince
and my religion be safe, I shall bless even my enemies
who do well for them, though in my ruin.'

" Then, with the advice of his friends, whose
counsel he always asked in cases of difficulty, he

* SEACOME'S *House of Stanley.*

despatched a messenger with letters to the King,"*
to assure him of his fidelity, declaring that, though
his enemies might prevent him from serving his
sovereign according to his birth and quality, " yet he
would never draw his sword against him; that he did
submissively resign the lieutenancies of Cheshire and
North Wales to his Majesty's disposal, but besought
him to take away that of Lancashire also, rather than
subject him to the reproach and suspicion of a partner
in that government." *

By this frank submission Lord Strange obtained
the removal of Lord Rivers, and secured for himself
the sole command of Lancashire.   But the country
gentlemen and the friends and dependants of the
house of Derby were not all so high-minded as
their chief; the ill-usage to which he had been
subjected was highly resented by them, and proved
of the greatest prejudice to the King's affairs in the
counties both of Lancashire and Cheshire.   Many
gentlemen retired to their country seats, resolved not
to risk their lives and property in the service of a
Prince who knew so ill how to reward the zeal of his
subjects.   Others, in great numbers, went over to the
Parliament, foreseeing that these counties, being
deprived of their hereditary leader, would never take

* Seacome's *House of Stanley.*

up arms in the royal cause ; and that, in the end, the Parliament would triumph in a part of the country which had at first seemed wholly devoted to the King.

The discontent was, indeed, so decided that the Commons offered Lord Strange an appointment in their army, or whatever power he chose in the county ; but he rejected the offer with indignation, and prepared at once to rejoin the King, who had set up his standard at Nottingham on the 28th of August, 1642, and who had written to recall him with his own hand.

Although Lord Strange's authority was still considerable in Cheshire and Lancashire, yet the position of affairs had greatly changed within the last two months. He represented to the King that, the Parliament having seized upon Manchester, many gentlemen of the county had joined them, while others had declared their intention of remaining neutral ; and that he could not venture upon a general muster of the county even in those parts which had remained faithful, so greatly had he suffered from the suspicions of which he had been the object. He was forced to be content with raising amongst his own relations, friends, and tenants three regiments of foot and three troops of horse ; and these he equipped and armed at his own expense, hastening with them to the King at Shrewsbury as soon as they were ready to march, that he might receive his commands for their disposal.

The King ordered them to attack Manchester, and desired Lord Strange to send the necessary instructions to Colonel Gilbert Gerrard, one of his lieutenants, and an experienced soldier. The rivers were so swollen that the march of the troops proceeded slowly, and Lord Strange (who had now just become Earl of Derby) was despatched to Manchester by the King's express command, with orders to hurry on the assault in person.

On his arrival before the town he summoned the rebels to surrender upon honourable terms; but his proposals were obstinately rejected, and he was preparing for an attack on the following day when letters arrived from Shrewsbury during the night, informing him that the Parliamentary army was then on its march from London, under the command of Lord Essex; that the King stood in need of all his forces to oppose the rebels; "that, if the town was not carried, he should not hazard any of them by an assault; that, if the King carried the battle against Essex, those small garrisons would fall of themselves; and that his Lordship should, on receipt of these letters, forthwith advance to him with what forces he had."*

* SEACOME'S *House of Stanley*.

Painful as it was to him, Lord Derby did not hesitate to obey the King's commands. To the regret of all his officers and soldiers, he left a place which he felt sure that he could have reduced at the first assault,—left it without striking a single blow. He began his march at five the next morning, and in two days arrived at Shrewsbury with his three regiments of infantry and three troops of horse, intending to form them into a brigade for the King's service.

But he had reckoned without his host—not remembering his enemies at Court. (The chronicler nowhere betrays the names of these enemies; but pursues them with his hatred under cover of the anonymous.) The King's mind had been already prejudiced against him, and soon after his arrival the command of the troops which he had himself raised, paid, and armed was taken from him, and bestowed upon other officers. Charles gave him no other reason for this act of injustice than that the duties of the Earl's office necessitated his presence in Lancaster, whither he was desired to hasten, and do all in his power to watch the movements and check the progress of the rebels in that county.

" The Earl, though a person of great temper," says his biographer, " was yet of as great a spirit. He was so ruffled at this unkind usage that he could scarce contain himself; but in a little time, recovering from his great surprise and concern, he replied to the King :—

" ' Sir, if I have deserved this indignity, I deserve also to be hanged; if not, my honour and quality command me to beg your justice against those persons who, in this insolent manner, abuse both me and your Majesty. And if any man living (your Majesty excepted) shall dare to fix the least accusation upon me that may tend to your disservice, I hope you will give me leave to pick the calumny from his lips with the point of my sword.'

" The King, with a smooth countenance, appeared to entertain no displeasure against his Lordship; but said :—

" ' My Lord, my affairs are troubled; the rebels are marching against me, and it is not now a time to quarrel amongst ourselves. Have a little patience, and I will do you right.' "*

The Earl was silent, and restrained his anger; but the treatment he had received could not be kept secret. A report of the matter soon spread through the army; his soldiers, draughted into other regiments, bluntly refused to serve; his friends murmured, and he saw that he must interfere. The King had

* SEACOME'S *House of Stanley.*

said truly that this was not a time for the Royalists to quarrel amongst themselves. He, therefore, exerted himself to calm the irritation of his friends; and when he left Shrewsbury for Latham House he had prevailed on his soldiers to serve the King dutifully, as he should himself do, notwithstanding what had happened.

The Parliamentarians in Lancashire very soon learnt that Lord Derby had reason to complain of his treatment at Court, and thinking this a fit moment to make another effort to attach him to their party, they sent him a letter containing fresh offers from the Parliament, in nearly the following words:

" That he could not but be very sensible of the indignity put upon him at Court by the King's evil counsellors; that those enemies were the enemies of the nation; that they struck at religion and all good men, and would permit none but Papists, or people popishly affected, to be near his Majesty; that it was the whole intent of the Parliament to remove men of such desperate and pernicious principles from his person, and to secure the true Protestant religion; and that if his Lordship would engage in that good cause, he should have command equal to his own greatness, or any of his ancestors." *

* SEACOME'S *House of Stanley.*

Lord Derby had restrained his anger before the King at Shrewsbury, but he could not contain himself on receipt of this message from the Parliament. Without giving himself the trouble of writing, he said to the Colonel who delivered the letter :

" Pray tell the gentlemen at Manchester, and let them tell the gentlemen at London, when they hear I turn traitor, I shall hearken to their propositions ; till then, if I receive any other papers of this nature, it shall be at the peril of him that brings them."*

By this time the Earl of Essex was at the head of his army, while the King was still engaged in raising forces to oppose him. Towards the end of September, the Parliamentary troops numbered about twenty thousand men, and those of the King nearly twelve thousand. Charles gave the command of his cavalry to Prince Rupert, who had just arrived from Germany, and who, daring and unprincipled, brave, and accustomed to the rudeness of German warfare, overran the country, pillaging and ravaging in all directions, and bringing the King's cause into bad repute with the people, without rendering him much service in the field.

Charles had resolved to march direct upon

* SEACOME'S *House of Stanley.*

London, and put an end to the war at one blow; Essex, who had advanced as far as Worcester, turned back to intercept him, and the two armies came up with each other at Edgehill, on the 23rd of October, 1642, where a fierce engagement took place, with, however, no decisive advantage on either side. The next day the King found that his army was too much weakened to renew the attack. Hampden, Hollis, and Stapleton pressed Essex to risk another engagement, but their advice was opposed by the military commanders: Essex therefore fell back upon Warwick, and the King established his head-quarters at Oxford, of all the large towns in the kingdom the one most devoted to his cause.

For a short time his affairs seemed to improve: many towns opened their gates to him; at Brentford, only three hours' march from London, a slight engagement took place. But it was now the middle of November; warlike operations were becoming difficult, and the King returned to Oxford, where he took up his winter quarters.

While the two principal armies remained thus inactive, several expeditions of little importance were attempted in various parts of the country. In some places confederations were formed, holding commissions either from the King or the Parliament, according to their several views. In others, influential noblemen or wealthy country gentlemen equipped bodies of men at their own expense, and carried on a warfare in their immediate neighbourhood, in the name of the party which they had embraced.

On one occasion Lord Derby defeated three such companies of infantry, who had advanced within six miles of Latham on their march across the country to join the Parliamentary army. This exploit made some noise, and brought reinforcements to the little body of men that he had again gathered together with infinite difficulty; for he had been left entirely without arms and ammunition, after having twice given up his stores to the King.

He now occupied himself in fortifying his own house at Latham, taking especial care to supply the castle with provisions, and troops for the defence of his wife and children, whom he left there during his distant journeys; for he was obliged to be constantly in the field, forcing the Parliamentarians to remain shut up in the towns which they had seized, the number of which was rapidly increasing.

In the beginning of March, 1643, Lord Molyneux came into Lancashire to recruit his regiment, which had only lately been formed out of the troops brought by Lord Derby to Shrewsbury, and which had been much shattered at Edgehill. Lord Derby immediately applied to him for assistance to besiege the Parliamentary garrisons at Lancaster and Preston. Lord Molyneux consenting, they left Latham House on the 17th of March, at nightfall, and, after a forced march of about thirty miles, the little army appeared the next morning before the walls of Lancaster. The garrison was summoned to surrender, and indignantly refused; the soldiers hesitated to make a second attack, when the Earl of Derby, seizing a short pike, sprang forward, crying, "Follow me!" Some gentlemen volunteers immediately joined him, and urged the soldiers on. The assault was made, the city taken, and the fortifications razed. Allowing the troops but a few days for rest, Lord Derby marched on Preston, and reduced it also on the 21st of March.

The value of this success was considerably diminished by the obstinate resistance of the town of Manchester, which was occupied by a body of fierce Parliamentarians. Lord Derby had proposed to make the attack while the alarm of the enemy was still fresh, in order to encourage those friends whom the King had in the place. He promised, if Lord Molyneux would continue to give him his co-operation, to take Manchester, or leave his bones there. Lord Molyneux at first refused; then, yielding to Lord Derby's

arguments, he apparently consented to accompany
him, and during the night the little army advanced as
far as Chorley ; but they had scarcely reached that
place when an express from Oxford ordered Lord
Molyneux to rejoin the King immediately.   Lord
Derby, in despair, begged for a delay.   Four days
would suffice to take Manchester,—his Majesty would
pardon the detention in consideration of so great a
success.   But Lord Molyneux and his officers were
inflexible.   At length, pushed to extremity by the
importunity of the Earl, they produced their commissions authorising them to recruit their regiments
from the troops that the Earl had just levied in
Lancashire.

The blow was sharp, and the insult evident.   Lord
Derby saw himself not only deprived of his auxiliaries
just when their aid was most needed for the King's
service ; but, for the second time, the troops he had
raised with so much difficulty, equipped and trained at
his own expense—those very men who had just given
so striking a proof of their valour—were taken from
him.   There was nothing now for him to do but to
retire to Latham, leaving the Parliamentarians to
attack the little town of Wigan, in which he had
recently placed a garrison under the command of
Major-General Blair, a Scotchman, who had been

recommended to him by the King. Wigan was taken and pillaged—the communion cups even were carried off from the church, and one of the Puritan preachers hung them round his neck as the spoil of idolatry.

So much contumely might well have crushed the strongest heart; but a deep sense of duty and of the goodness of his cause upheld the Earl. He silenced the murmurs that rose around him against the injustice of the Court, and repeated the fine passage from Tacitus : " *Pravis dictis factisque ex posteritate et fama metus.*"

There was fighting in all parts of the country, though the war could not properly be said to have recommenced, nor the struggle to have yet become characterized by any violent animosity. In the middle of February the arrival of the Queen gave affairs a new impulse. She landed at Burlington, and was received by the Duke of Newcastle, who conducted her to York, where she stationed herself. There was much stir at her Court. Hamilton and Montrose had returned from Scotland full of schemes for bringing over that kingdom to the King's side; while, at the same time, the Queen herself was carrying on negotiations with certain of the Parliamentary leaders who had become weary of their cause. The hopes of the Royalists were reviving everywhere in the North.

Proposals for resuming negotiations of peace were made to Parliament; and, in spite of their secret anger, the Commons were obliged to send five Commissioners to Oxford for twenty days to arrange, first, a suspension of arms, and afterwards a treaty of peace. But all this was rendered of no effect by the King's obstinacy, aided as it was by the manœuvres of those adherents of the Queen who wanted no negotiations to be entered into without her sanction. The King finished by declaring to the Commissioners that he was willing to return to the Parliament if they would transfer their place of sitting to twenty miles at least from London. At this repulse, the Parliament recalled their Commissioners by so peremptory a message that they had not time to wait for their carriages, but left the same day on horseback. They reached London as Essex opened the campaign of 1643.

CHAPTER IV.

THE SIEGE OF LATHAM HOUSE.

WHILE the negotiations were going on at Oxford, the Earl of Derby, who had returned to Latham, and was trying to muster new forces for the King's service, received an express from Charles to the effect that his enemies had formed a project to seize the Isle of Man; that they had a party in the island in confederacy with them, and that without speedy care it was in danger of being lost. The King thanked him for his loyal services in England, and urged him to direct his efforts towards preserving the Isle of Man by proceeding thither as fast as possible.*

The Earl was not deceived with regard to the purport of this advice when he read the despatch. He exclaimed to his wife, with more than ordinary quickness, "My heart, my enemies have now their

---

* SEACOME'S *House of Stanley.*

will, having prevailed with his Majesty to order me
to the Isle of Man, as a softer banishment from his
presence and their malice." *

For the first time the Earl hesitated to obey. " I,"
he said, " that have, with the few that durst take my
part, hitherto kept the greater part of Lancashire in
subjection to his Majesty, in spite of his enemies, must
now abandon my family, friends, and country's safety
to the malice of a wicked multitude, without either
mercy or compassion." *

In the *History of the House of Stanley*, written
by Scacome, the steward of Lord Derby, grandson
of Earl James, we find at this time some fragments
of the Earl's memoirs :—" It being now known,"
he writes, " that the Queen was at York with great
forces, I was advised and requested by the loyal
gentlemen then with me, to go to her Majesty, and
represent to her our distressed state, and the necessity
of giving us speedy help and relief; which I complied
with, leaving the few forces I had in Lancashire under
command of Lord Molyneux, who gave me in the
end as much trouble as the enemy ; and I set out
for York." *

Essex had taken Reading from the King's troops,
and Hampden urged him to besiege Oxford; but

* SEACOME'S *House of Stanley.*

the General refused. He had engaged in the war
unwillingly, and he was not quite sure of his army.

The King's cause began to look more hopeful.
An important plot in his favour had been discovered
in London ; and, though the persons engaged in it had
been severely punished, the fact of the plot existing in
the heart of the City alarmed the Parliament. A fresh
blow extinguished the confidence and well nigh the
hopes of the whole party. On the 19th of June
Hampden was wounded in a cavalry skirmish with
Prince Rupert. " I saw him," said a prisoner, " quit
the field before the action was finished, contrary to
his custom; his head was hanging down, his hands
leaning on his horse's neck."   Five days after, on
the 24th of June, Hampden expired at the age of
forty-nine,—suddenly cut off from all the hopes, and
escaping alike the perils and the crimes, of the future.
" Happy and but too rare fortune, which thus fixed
his name for ever on that height whither the love
and full confidence of his contemporaries had carried
it, and perhaps saved his virtue, like his glory, from
the rocks on which revolutions drive and wreck the
noblest of their favourites." *

With the death of Hampden fortune seemed to
desert his party. Lord Fairfax, father of Sir Thomas,

* Guizot's *History of the English Revolution.*

was defeated at Atherton Moor, in the North; Sir John Hotham was on the point of surrendering Hull to the Queen; Lord Willoughby declared he could no longer defend Lincolnshire against the Duke of New-castle; Sir William Waller had been twice beaten in one week. The triumphant Queen was preparing to join the King at Oxford.

She had promised forces to the Earl of Derby to enable him to hold the county of Lancaster; but the frivolous courtiers who surrounded her had no sympathy with the proud and austere nobleman who was indifferent to their good graces, but served his Sovereigns without favour or baseness. "A vexatious accident," says the Earl in his memoirs—"the defeat of Lord Goring at Wakefield," says Captain Halsall,* to whom we are indebted for the narrative of the siege of Latham, "prevented the troops from being sent off."

"In my absence," continues the Earl, "the enemy possessed themselves of the whole country, saving my house and Sir John Girlington's . . . . and my troops taking a march towards York in hopes of meeting me there, were disappointed : which verified the old proverb, 'Ill fortune seldom comes alone.' For at that

* *Journal of the Siege of Latham House.* By Captain EDWARD HALSALL.

time a report was spread that some Scots, intending
to assist the Parliament, would land in the north, and
in their way endeavour to take the Isle of Man."

The Earl of Derby, however, did not give much
heed to this rumour, and retained his desire to
accompany the Queen to Oxford, where the King
was ; but his Majesty had other views, as the Earl
wrote to his son, Lord Strange, in the memoir we
have already quoted from : " I had received letters
from the Isle of Man intimating the great danger of a
revolt there ; for that many people, following the
example of England, began by murmuring and com-
plaining against the Government, and from some
seditious and wicked spirits had learned the same
lessons with the Londoners, to come to Court in a
tumultuous manner, demanding new laws, and a change
of the old ; that they would have no Bishops, pay no
tithes to the clergy ; despised authority, and rescued
some who had been committed by the Governor
for insolence and contempt. It was also reported
that a ship of war, which I had there for a defence
of the island, was taken by the Parliament's ships;
which proved true. And that it was judged by the
Queen and those with her, (as Lord Goring, Lord
Digby, Lord Jermin, Sir Edward Deering, and many
more,) that I should forthwith go to the island to

prevent the impending mischief in time, as well for the King's service, as the preservation of my own inheritance."

This resolution, which cost the Earl so much, was attributed by his enemies to a cowardly desire to withdraw himself from the struggle. "It has been said," he writes in his memoir, in a letter to his son, "that I wished to become neutral, and many such like invidious and malicious suggestions to my prejudice. But, I bless God, I am fully satisfied with my own conduct and integrity of heart, well remembering all those circumstances, as well as the wicked insinuations of my implacable and restless enemies.

"How others may be satisfied herewith I know not, but think this short relation, for want of time to set things in a fuller light, may rather puzzle the minds of the readers, if any should chance to see it but yourself; but you, my son, are bound to believe well of your father, and I to be thankful to Almighty God that you so well understand yourself and me: as for others, I am unconcerned whether they understand me or not.

"Upon the above advice by the Queen and friends, I returned to Latham; and having secretly made what provisions I possibly could of men, money, and ammunition, for the defence and protection of my wife and

children against the insolence and affronts of the
enemy, prepared for my speedy voyage to the Isle of
Man, taking with me such men and materials as
might answer those purposes I was sent about.

" Leaving my house and children, and all my
concerns in England to the care of my wife, a person
of virtue and honour equal to her high birth and
quality, who being now left alone, a woman, a stranger
in the country, and (as the enemy thought) without
friends, provisions, or ammunition, for defence or resistance, concluded that Latham House would fall an
easy prey to them ; to which purpose they procured a
commission from the Parliament to reduce it by treaty
or force." *

The Earl had scarcely left England when Lady
Derby received proposals from Mr. Holland, Governor
of Manchester for the Parliament, which she was called
on either to accept, or to surrender her house. Her
reply was not what was expected. " It did not suit her,"
she said, " either humbly to give up her house, or to
purchase repose at the price of honour." Lord Derby's
efforts, however, had not succeeded in furnishing the
house with sufficient provisions and ammunition for a
long siege, and the Countess therefore asked to be
permitted to remain in peace at Latham, giving up the

* SEACOME's *House of Stanley.*

land entirely to the good pleasure of the Parliament, and reserving only for herself a sufficient garrison of men at arms to protect herself and her household from the insults of the soldiers. She obtained this favour with great difficulty.

For eight months she remained a prisoner in her house and park, rarely going beyond the courts that surrounded the house lest she should meet with some affront. Deprived of the revenues of her estates, attacked by her friends as well as by her enemies,— the first reproaching her for not having defended her property and her liberty, the last blaming her for not giving up to the Parliament the house as well as the domain,—she waited patiently for the time when she should be able openly to resist. Steadily and secretly she had collected provisions and ammunition, bringing in the men one by one, and the barrels of powder in the night; repressing the zeal of her garrison, who longed to revenge the insults she had to submit to daily; and preparing herself in silence for the siege which she foresaw must come. In so proud a nature as hers, this noble patience resulted from even a higher courage than Lady Derby displayed in the midst of armed attacks,—the courage of a woman and of a general who knows how to bear all while awaiting the time to dare all.

"Latham House," writes Samuel Rutter, the Earl of Derby's chaplain, afterwards Archdeacon, and finally Bishop of Man, "stands on a flat, upon a moorish spongy ground; was encompassed with a strong wall two yards thick; upon the walls were nine towers flanking each other; and in every tower were six pieces of ordnance, that played three one way and three the other. Without the wall was a moat, eight yards wide, and two yards deep; upon the back of the moat, between the wall and the graff, was a strong wall of palisades around; besides all these there was a high, strong tower, called the Eagle Tower, in the midst of the house surmounting all the rest; and the gate-house was also two high and strong buildings, with a strong tower on each side of it. . . . Besides all that is said hitherto of the walls, tower, moat, &c., there is something particular and romantic in the general situation of this house, as if nature herself had formed it for a stronghold or place of security. . . . . The uncommon situation of it may be compared to the palm of a man's hand, flat in the middle, and covered with a rising round about it; and so near to it, that the enemy in two years were never able to raise a battery against it so as to make a breach in the wall practicable to enter the house by way of storm."[*]

* SEACOME'S *House of Stanley.*

The Countess's preparations were nearly completed, in spite of the difficulties incessantly put in
her way by Colonel Rigby, who commanded the
Parliamentary troops in that neighbourhood. It was
in vain that he had pillaged the houses of her
adherents, and arrested the people who came to seek
refuge at Latham. Lady Derby had succeeded in
getting into the house more than three hundred
men, and a great abundance of food of all kinds.
Ammunition, however, was less considerable, and
they were obliged to economize their powder. Lady
Derby commanded in chief, says Captain Halsall,
but to make up for her ignorance of military matters,
she had with her a Scotchman, Captain Farmer, whom
she had made major of her house, and six lieutenants
chosen from the gentlemen of the neighbourhood who
had come to offer their services.

The garrison had been gathered together with so
much secrecy that the Parliamentarians had no idea of
its strength ; and, after a slight engagement between
the troops of Colonel Rigby and those of the Countess,
Sir Thomas Fairfax resolved to deliver the county of
Lancaster from this nest of delinquents.

It was decided in the council of war held at
Manchester on the 24th of February, 1644, that three
Colonels,—Ashton of Midleton, Moor of Bank Hall,

and Rigby of Preston,—should attack Latham House. This was on Saturday; and on Sunday morning rumours of the projected movement reached the Countess. She sent in haste to a friend on whom she could rely to obtain full information ; and in the mean-time hurried forward her final preparations, rendered doubly difficult by the ill-will of some of her tenants who inclined to the popular cause, and considered that the sequestration had released them from all obligation to the mistress of the house and domain. But it was not in vain that Lady Derby belonged to the proud race of French Huguenots whose power had once kept that of Royalty in the balance; it was not in vain that the blood of William of Nassau flowed in her veins. She was equal to her position; she watched over everything; calm and resolute, she assigned to every man his post, singling out the best marksmen, those who had been accustomed to attend the Earl in his hunting, to occupy the towers of the gate-house for the purpose of harrassing and annoying the enemy. Then, when everything was arranged, all the soldiers were ordered to disappear from the ramparts, and the Countess, apparently alone with her household, awaited the visit that had been announced.

The Parliamentary soldiers had not been made

aware that they were marching against Latham
House; perhaps the leaders feared the hereditary
attachment of the people of Lancashire to that noble
family who had for so many years held an actual court
in the midst of them, dispensing a princely hospitality
and an inexhaustible charity. While it was known to
the Countess that the Parliamentary army was *en
route*, by Bolton, Wigan, and Standish, the people
believed that they were advancing towards Westmore-
land; but those who went to church at Wigan were
undeceived, for one of the preachers taking for his
text Jeremiah, l. 14, " Put yourselves in array against
Babylon round about : all ye that bend the bow shoot
at her, spare no arrows; for she hath sinned against
the Lord," compared the Countess of Derby to Babylon, the great city of the Apocalypse, and announced
his intention of reserving the following verse : " Shout
against her round about : she hath given her hand :
her foundations are fallen, her walls are thrown down,"
for the text of the sermon that should celebrate the
victory over her.

On the 27th February the enemy took up their
quarters two miles from Latham, and on the 28th
Capt. Markland arrived at the house with a letter
from Sir Thomas Fairfax, and an order from the
Parliament promising grace to Lord Derby if he

submitted. Sir Thomas Fairfax engaged to carry out this promise faithfully, and called on the Countess to surrender Latham House to him on honourable conditions, which he would make known to her. The letter was courteous, as from a gentleman to a lady of high rank and reputation; but the Countess felt the necessity of gaining time: her troops were inexperienced, and the training they received from their captains increased their courage and confidence daily. Her reply to Sir Thomas Fairfax, therefore, was to the effect that "She much wondered that Sir Thomas Fairfax should require her to give up her lord's house, without any offence on her part done to the Parliament; desiring that in a business of such weight, which struck both at her religion and her life, and that so nearly concerned her sovereign, her lord, and her whole posterity, she might have a week's consideration, to resolve the doubts of conscience, and to have advice in matters of law and honour." *

Sir Thomas Fairfax probably thought Lady Derby's conscience sufficiently enlightened, for he refused to give her the time she asked, and invited her to go in her carriage to New Park, a house belonging to Lord Derby, situated a short distance from Latham, in order to have an interview with him and

* HALSALL's *Siege of Latham House.*

his Colonels for the free discussion of the whole affair.

When the Countess received this letter it roused the haughtiness of the great lady as well as the boldness of the heroine. "Say to Sir Thomas Fairfax," said she, "that, notwithstanding my present position, I do not forget either the honour of my lord or my own birth, and that I conceive it more knightly that Sir Thomas Fairfax should wait upon me than I upon him."

Two days passed in letters and in messages; at length the General demanded free entrance to Latham House for two of his Colonels; and the Countess promised to allow them to return in safety. They came on the 2nd of March; but the house that lately had the appearance of being peaceably occupied by women and children, with old servants and a few men at arms for protection, had now assumed the appearance of a fortress. Lady Derby had suddenly unmasked her batteries, either from fear of an immediate attack, or to produce an imposing effect on the enemy. A body of soldiers well equipped, ranged under orders of their lieutenants, formed a line from the first court to the great hall into which the Parliamentary officers were introduced: the towers and ramparts were bristling with men; the cannon were uncovered ; everything wore a martial appearance, and throughout perfect discipline prevailed. At the end of the great hall, more imposing than all her forces sat the general of this little army, the Countess of Derby, surrounded by her women, and with her two daughters beside her. She waited for the officers to approach ; then, making a sign to them to be seated with the manner of a sovereign who gives an audience she listened to the propositions of Sir Thomas. They were as follows :—

" 1. That all the arms and ammunition of war shall be forthwith surrendered into the hands of Sir Thomas Fairfax.

" 2. That the Countess of Derby, and all the persons in Latham House, shall be suffered to depart with all their goods to Chester, or any other of the enemy's quarters, or, upon submission to the order of Parliament, to their own houses.

" 3. That the Countess with all her menial servants shall be suffered either to inhabit Knowsley House, and to have twenty muskets allowed for her defence, or to repair to her husband in the Isle of Man.

" 4. That the Countess for the present, until the Parliament be acquainted with it, shall have allowed her for her maintenance all the lands and revenues (

the Earl her husband within the hundred of Derby, and that the Parliament shall be moved to continue this allowance.

" These conditions her Ladyship rejected as being in part dishonourable, and in part uncertain; adding withall, she knew not how to treat with them who had not power to perform their own offers till they had first moved the Parliament, telling them that it were a more sober course first to acquaint themselves with the pleasure of the Parliament, and then to move accordingly; but for her part she would not trouble the good gentlemen to petition for her; she would esteem it a greater favour to be permitted to continue in her present humble condition."*

The two Colonels did not insist. For some time past Rigby had been eager to take revenge for an insult which he believed he had received from the Earl. They had indeed read determination in the lady's eyes; yet they could not let themselves be thus conquered by a woman, and they both thought it necessary to address some representations to her on the error of her ways, and to reproach her with the wrong-doing attributed in the country to her friends and servants. " I shall know how to take care of my ways and those of my house," said the Countess gravely; " you

* HALSALL'S *Siege of Latham House.*

would do well to do as much for your ministers and
agents of religion who go about sowing discord and
trouble in families, whose unbridled tongues do not spare
even the sacred person of his Majesty." Henry Martyn
might say to the Parliament, "the ruin of one single
family is better than the ruin of many;" and when they
asked him of whom he spoke he could answer without
hesitation, "of the King and his family;" but the
lieutenants of Fairfax knew that their General would
not have permitted such language, and "the grave
men, being disappointed both of their wit and malice,
returned as empty as they came." *

Sunday was a day of rest for the besiegers as well
as for the besieged. While they preached against
her in the camp of Fairfax, probably with sincerity
equal to her own, the Countess of Derby, with her
children and the greater part of the garrison, was
present at divine service in the chapel of the house,
where four times a day during the siege she made the
chaplain offer prayers; she herself always attending,
and gathering new strength for her heavy task at the
feet of Him who has called Himself the Lord of
Hosts.

"On Monday Mr. Ashton came again, alone, with
power to receive her Ladyship's propositions, and to

* HALSALL'S *Siege of Latham House.*

convey them to his General, which came in these terms :—

" 1. Her Ladyship desired a month's time for her quiet continuance in Latham; and then, for herself and children, her friends, soldiers, and servants, with all her goods, arms, and ordnance, to have free transport to the Isle of Man, and in the meantime that she should keep a garrison in her house for her own defence.

" 2. She promised that neither during her stay in the country, nor after her coming to the Isle of Man, should any of the arms be employed against the Parliament.

" 3. That during her stay in the country, no soldier should be quartered in the lordship of Latham, nor afterwards should any garrison be put into Latham or into Knowsley House.

" 4. That none of her tenants, neighbours, or friends, then in the house with her, should, for assisting her, suffer in their persons or estates, after her departure." *

Fairfax was not deceived by these proposals. He understood that the Countess only wished to gain time for victualling her house ; and he foresaw that she would elude the clause in which she promised not to

* HALSALL'S *Siege of Latham House.*

bear arms against the Parliament, by referring herself to the Parliament of the three estates—King, Lords, and Commons, then assembled at Oxford. For the last time, therefore, he sent counter-propositions :—

" 1. The Countess of Derby shall have the time that she desires, and then liberty to transport her arms and goods to the Isle of Man, excepting the cannon, which shall continue there for the defence of the place.

" 2. That her Ladyship, by ten o'clock to-morrow, disband all her soldiers, except her menial servants, and receive an officer and forty Parliament soldiers as her guard." *

A new messenger was the bearer of this new message, Colonel Morgan, a hot-headed Welshman, with a sharp, imperative manner, who was, however, obliged to restrain himself before the pride and dignity of the Countess, who sent back this last answer :—

" That she refused all their articles, and was truly happy that they had refused hers, protesting that she would rather hazard her life than offer the like again. That though a woman and a stranger, divorced from her friends, and robbed of her estate, she was ready to receive their utmost violence, trusting in God both for protection and deliverance." *

* HALSALL'S *Siege of Latham House.*

Negotiations being thus closed, Captain Morgan went off into descriptions of the cannon, mortars, bombs, and artillery, that would be brought against the house, and left the Countess to reflect on the danger she had so proudly braved.

The council of war met. Some of the Parliamentary officers advised an immediate assault; others, a regular siege. The person who supported this last proposal most earnestly was a captain who, in his childhood, had been closely associated with the Rev. Mr. Rutter, the Countess's chaplain, with whom he had had a conversation on the occasion of the late conference with Lady Derby. From what had passed then he believed that the house was but scantily victualled, for not more than twelve or fifteen days; and that the Countess eagerly desired an assault. They therefore resolved on the siege, and on the 7th of March began to open a trench, in which labour the country people were forced to take an active part.

The works went on round the house, and the circle was growing rapidly, when Lady Derby was informed that six of her neighbours of the highest rank desired to speak with her. She ordered them to be admitted, and received them with her customary courtesy.

At the first glance she detected the origin of the

petition they brought. It proceeded from the Parliament, and the worthy delegates had been carefully instructed. "In duty to her Ladyship and love to their country they most humbly besought her to prevent her own personal dangers and the impoverishing of the whole country, which she might do if she pleased to slacken something of her severe resolution, and to condescend in part to the offers of the gentlemen."*

The Countess did not receive her neighbours with the same haughtiness which she had shown to the emissaries of the Parliament. She explained her reasons for rejecting the preceding propositions, and advised them to address their petition to the men who robbed and spoiled their country, rather than to her who desired no other favour than to remain at home in peace. The good men were satisfied, and had little more to say than "God save the King and the Earl of Derby."

The report they gave of the interview to Sir Thomas Fairfax decided him to send Captain Ashurst the next day to Latham House with new propositions. "This Captain Ashurst," says Captain Halsall, "deserves a fairer character than the rest for his civil and even behaviour. His new message to her Ladyship was in these terms :—

* HALSALL's *Siege of Latham House.*

" 1. That all former conditions be waived.

" 2. That the Countess of Derby and all persons in the house, with all arms, ordnance, and goods, shall have liberty to march to what part of the kingdom they please, and yield up the house to Sir Thomas Fairfax.

" 3. That the arms shall never be employed against the Parliament.

" 4. That all in the house except a hundred persons should immediately leave it, and the rest in ten days." *

Fairfax was evidently unwilling to attack the place, either because he considered the enterprise a difficult one, or because he was ashamed to employ his arms against a woman, defending her children and her husband's house. But the Countess showed no fear. The reply she sent to the General was, " That, as she had not lost her regard for the Church of England, nor her allegiance to her prince, nor her faith to her lord, she could not therefore, as yet, give up that house; that they must never hope to gain it till she had either lost all these, or her life in defence of them." †

Fairfax had now nothing to do but to begin the

---

* HALSALL'S *Siege of Latham House.*
† SEACOME'S *House of Stanley.*

siege in good earnest. The trenches around Latham progressed daily, notwithstanding the continual sorties made by the garrison on the men who were at work there. One small detachment of cavalry even fought hand to hand with some Parliamentary troops, and brought back a few prisoners, from whom it was ascertained that the blockade was determined on; "the Commanders," says Captain Halsall, "having courage to pine a lady, not to fight with her."

The work of the siege was proceeding rapidly, to the great injury of the country people employed in removing the earth, when, on the 20th March, Sir Thomas Fairfax sent the Countess a letter, which he had just received from her husband.

Alarmed at his wife's critical position, the Earl of Derby wrote from the Isle of Man asking the General to permit the Countess and her children freely to leave the house, in order to spare them the horrors of a siege, "especially considering the roughness and inhumanity of the enemy : . . . . not knowing, by reason of his long absence, either how his house was provided with victuals and ammunition, or strengthened for resistance. He was therefore desirous to leave only the hardy soldiers for the brunt,—' if it seems good to my wife,'" added he. But it did not seem good to the courageous daughter of the Nassaus. Her spirit rose at the approach of danger, and if her heart beat at this proof of the tender solicitude of her husband, she derived from it fresh strength to remain at the post which he had entrusted to her. She bade the messenger, a coarse preacher employed by Colonel Rigby, say to Sir Thomas Fairfax that she thanked him for his courtesy : " that she would willingly submit herself to her lord's commands, and therefore willed the General to treat with him ; but, till she was assured that such was his lordship's pleasure, she would neither yield up the house, nor desert it herself, but wait for the event according to the will of God." *

She had meanwhile learned that her husband had quitted the Isle of Man, and she had taken advantage of a sortie, which threw the enemy into confusion and put them off their guard, to despatch an express to him at Chester, where he was anxiously and busily collecting forces with which to march in person to the help of his family. But the house was surrounded by 3,000 men, and the Earl had barely a handful of soldiers.

Meanwhile the sorties of the garrison of Latham continued ; and the cannon began to batter the walls of the House, but, thanks to the nature of the ground, not very effectually.

* HALSALL'S *Siege of Latham House.*

The garrison were anxiously watching the erection of a mortar that the enemy was placing on a mound, at the distance of half a gun-shot. The first shots passed over the house, to the great relief of the besieged, who had been furnished by the Countess with the wet hides of newly-killed animals with which to extinguish any fire that might occur.

Four days of prayer and pious exercises interrupted the operations of the siege; "four days of sleep," says the historian of Latham, incredulous as to the devotion of Colonel Rigby. At the end of that time the garrison determined to awaken the besiegers by a furious sortie, in which they spiked several of their cannon, and took a great number of prisoners, whom the Countess, proud of having scarcely any men left in the hands of the enemy, would have consented to release in exchange for some of the king's friends detained at Manchester, Preston, and Lancaster. Colonel Rigby promised this : but failed to fulfil his engagement, "it suiting well their religion," says the narrator of the siege, "neither to observe faith with God nor with men." And then followed at Latham a melancholy massacre of prisoners whom the Countess could neither keep nor set free.

With her children—her two daughters, Mary and Catherine, -- she watched over every thing : arranged for the food of the soldiers—was present at the distribution of the powder—at the nursing of the wounded —was often on the ramparts, and always at chapel at prayer-time. When a bullet fell in her bed-room she smiled disdainfully, and it was only after the same thing had happened three or four times that she would condescend to change her apartment, though still with the " protest that she would keep the house while there was a single building to cover her head."

On one occasion a shell had burst in the dining-room during dinner, which broke the glass and furniture, but injured no one. The children were beside their mother at the time, but they did not move, and scarcely changed colour. The Countess merely gave them a look of approbation, and the meal was continued in the midst of the confusion.

On the 24th of April Sir Thomas Fairfax, who had till then directed the siege, grown tired of making war against a woman, left for York, abandoning the enterprise against Latham House to Colonel Rigby, who had managed to disembarrass himself of Colonel Egerton, hitherto associated with him in authority. The Colonels Moor, Holcroft, Holland, and Ashton were his subordinates; Colonel Morgan was at the head of the engineering. The siege had now changed

its character. The Countess had no longer to deal
with one who, though a sincere patriot, was a gentleman and a man of cultivation and refined feeling.
Her present assailant—formerly a lawyer—was a bad
man, a robber and a hypocrite. Resolved not to be
conquered by a woman, he laid in a new stock of
grenadoes, which he used so freely that the besieged
renewed their ammunition in the trenches; and he
announced a grand attack with mortar-piece and
cannon.

Before striking this terrible blow, however, Colonel
Rigby desired once more to offer the rebels a chance
of submission; and on the 25th an insolent message
was brought to the Countess, ordering her to surrender
herself, with her house, her garrison, her arms, and
ammunition, to the mercy of Parliament before two
o'clock the next day.

She was in the court-yard in the midst of her
lieutenants when the messenger arrived. She took
the letter and read it; "then," says Captain Halsall,
"with a brave indignation calls for the drum, and
tells him that a due reward for his pains is to be
hanged up at her gates; 'but,' says she, 'thou art but
the foolish instrument of a traitor's pride; carry this
answer back to Rigby,' (with a noble scorn tearing
the paper in his sight,) 'and tell that insolent rebel he

shall neither have persons, goods, nor house. When our strength and provision is spent we shall find a fire more merciful than Rigby's ; and then, if the providence of God prevent it not, my goods and house shall burn in his sight ; and myself, children, and soldiers, rather than fall into his hands, will seal our religion and loyalty in the same flame ;' which, being spoken aloud in her soldiers' hearing, they broke out into shouts and acclamations of joy, all closing with this general voice, 'We will die for his Majesty and your Honour—God save the King!'" *

The time had come for acting resolutely; from words it was necessary to proceed to actions. The mortar-piece was the terror of all the garrison. " The little ladies had stomachs to digest cannon," says Captain Halsall, "but the stoutest soldier had no heart for grenadoes." They had tried in vain to spike the mortar-piece, its mouth was too large to be shut. It was in vain that the best marksmen aimed at the artillerymen in charge of the terrible engine; they fell, indeed, but others replaced them immediately. It only remained to attack the mortar itself ; and a sortie was arranged for the next day before the firing began.

It was 4 o'clock in the morning when Captain

* HALSALL'S *Siege of Latham House.*

Chisenhall and his eighty men silently left the eastern
gate, and before they were perceived they were under
the cannon, and after a slight skirmish were masters of
the little fort that covered the house. In the meantime Captain Fox, who had gone out by another
gate, had made himself master of the works which
defended the mortar, in spite of a deep ditch and a
tolerably high rampart. The two main works being
thus obtained, the first care of the Captains was to
level the ditch, while Captain Ogle and his soldiers
beat back the enemy who were trying to recover
their position.

The servants of the Countess had gone out in
crowds, every one eager to have a hand on the ropes
which had been passed round the mortar, and to
help in drawing within the ramparts the terrible
enemy that had done them so much harm. Captain
Ogle with a detachment of soldiers protected the
passage against another company of the enemy.

At length, amid cries of joy from all the garrison,
and to the great consternation of the besiegers, the
formidable engine was rolled into the court-yard, to
the Countess's feet. She immediately ordered her
chaplain to be called, and gathered her household
together in the chapel, to return thanks to God. The
soldiers had tried to carry off the large guns, but found

them too heavy, and they contented themselves with spiking as many as they could. The enterprise had cost the lives of two of the garrison; the loss of the enemy was more considerable. During the heat of the action the most skilful marksmen placed on the walls of the house had kept up an incessant fire, to the great destruction of the Parliamentary soldiers, who were gathered in crowds round the fort and near the ditch.

The joy within the house was great; their enemy, the monster vomiting flames, which had so often set fire to the old parts of the house, lay there in the court, mute and inoffensive; and every one gave it a kick as if in revenge for the terror it had once occasioned.

An additional zest was imparted to their triumph by the circumstance that Rigby had invited his friends in the neighbourhood to come on this day and see the reduction or the burning of the house. They were invited for 2 o'clock, and his friends, says Captain Halsall, "came opportunely to comfort him who was sick of shame and dishonour, in being routed by a lady and a handful of men."

After this, discouragement and discontent increased amongst the besiegers; desertion began in their ranks. The sorties of the garrison were so frequent that the

Parliamentarians were obliged incessantly to mount a guard. Rigby complained of this in a letter which he addressed on the 1st of May to the Deputy-Lieutenant of the county of Lancaster, representing that, as the Colonels Ashton and Holland, with their troops, had left him, he was no longer equal to the task which had been given him. " We are obliged to drive them back as often as five or six times in the same night," he wrote. " These constant alarms, the strength of the garrison, and the numerous losses we have had, oblige the soldiers to guard the trenches sometimes two nights running, and always the whole of the two nights : my son does this duty, as well as the youngest officer. And, for my own part, I am ready to sink under the weight, having worked beyond my strength."

In answer to this remonstrance, Colonel Holland was sent from Manchester to Rigby's assistance.

The incessant rains of spring impeded the operations of the besiegers; the earth was loosened, their trench fell in, and they began to lose the hope of cutting off the water from the besieged, which they had been trying to do for a month.

On the 23rd of May, the besiegers, more weary than the besieged of this long and desperate struggle, which brought them neither honour nor profit, made

one more attempt to induce the Countess to surrender.
Captain Mosley presented himself at the gate of the
house, bearing a letter to her Ladyship from Colonels
Holland and Rigby, ordering her, with rather more
insolence than had been used to her before, (for " it
not befitting Colonel Rigby's greatness," says Captain
Halsall, " to abate any of his former demands,") " to
yield up her house, her arms, her goods, all her
servants, and her own person and children, into their
hands, to be submitted to the mercy of the Parliament; which being read, her Ladyship smiled, and
in a troubled passion challenged the Captain with a
mistake in the paper, saying *mercy*, instead of *cruelty.*
' No,' says he, ' the mercy of the Parliament ; ' when
her Ladyship quickly and composedly replied, ' The
mercies of the wicked are cruel. Not that I mean,'
says she, ' a wicked Parliament, of which body I have
an honourable and reverend esteem, but wicked factors
and agents, such as Moor and Rigby, who, for the
advantage of their own interests, labour to turn kingdoms into blood and ruin. That unless they would
treat with her lord, they should never have her, nor
any of her friends, alive.' " *

The Captain gave her to understand that she
could obtain the conditions she had at first asked

* HALSALL'S *Siege of Latham House.*

for, if she would leave the house. " Let that insolent
rebel send me no more propositions," said she, "or his
messenger shall be hanged at my gates;" which words
the soldiers heard with acclamations; and the envoy
returned without having obtained any other answer,
nor a single word from the hand of the Countess.

But deliverance was at hand, though Lady Derby
did not know it. Shut up within her walls, she knew
nothing of the movements of the King or of those of
the Earl of Essex: she had scarcely heard of the
efforts her husband was making in all parts to bring
her help. She had learned from the taunts of the
besiegers that Sir Thomas Fairfax had defeated a
numerous body of Royalists at Selby; that the Duke
of Newcastle was shut up in York; that a new army
had been raised in the east under Cromwell; and that
Sir William Waller had defeated Sir Ralph Hopton
in Hampshire. All these disasters were so many
arguments to induce the Countess to surrender. But
she did not put much faith in them, and would not
even believe when the men in the trench called out
the news that Essex was on the point of besieging
Oxford; and that the Queen, terrified at the prospect
of her accouchment taking place in a city surrounded
by the enemy, had left the King her husband, to go
and establish herself at Exeter. Lady Derby had no

sympathy with terrors of this kind, and smiled scorn-
fully when the reports were brought to her. But they
were nevertheless true.

While the King's Generals were being defeated in
various directions, Prince Rupert had succeeded in
raising the siege of Newark, and was preparing to
march to the aid of the Duke of Newcastle, who was
threatened in York by Fairfax, Manchester, and the
Scotch army, which had just arrived under command
of the Earl of Leven. The Earl of Derby conjured
the Prince to pass through the county of Lancaster,
and deliver Latham House, and his wife and children;
and to quicken the march of the army, he promised the
soldiers a reward of three thousand pounds, raised
on his wife's jewels, which she had found means of
conveying to him during the siege.

The Parliamentarians had known for several days
that the troops of the Royalists were advancing, when,
on the night of the 23rd of May, a few hours after
the departure of Captain Mosley, one of the Countess's
scouts succeeded in stealing into the house (not,
however, without having killed the enemy's sentinel),
with the intelligence from the Earl that Prince Rupert
had entered the county of Chester; that report said
the Earl of Derby was with him; and that they were
both marching to the succour of Latham.

This unlooked-for news transported the timid with
joy, but the strong were unmoved by it.   Prayer more
fervent than ever rose from the little chapel; but no
precaution was neglected, and no advantage given to
the enemy.

Gravely and silently the Parliamentarians guarded
their trench, no longer shouting out insulting tidings
to the besieged, as they had been wont to do.   No
one now boasted of the successes of Fairfax in
the North, or of those of Cromwell in the East;
nothing more was heard of taking the King in a
mousetrap.

In the evening of the 26th of May, the guard was
renewed in such small number that the Countess
determined to attempt a grand sortie the next day.
Captain Ogle and Captain Rawstorne were selected
for this service, with two hundred soldiers of the
garrison.

The besieged were to attack the trench at three
o'clock in the morning; but by one o'clock the enemy
had raised their camp, collected their forces, and
packed up their tents.

The news that Prince Rupert had entered the
county of Lancaster had arrived during the evening.
He had forced his way past Stockport, in spite of the
resistance of Colonel Duckenfeld, and Rigby, like a

brave general, sparing of the lives of his men, determined not to wait for his coming to Latham. By six in the morning he and his troops were on Eccleston Moor, six miles from Latham, much puzzled where to turn his steps : Colonel Holland had returned to Manchester, and Colonel Moor to Liverpool. At length, thinking Prince Rupert was going through Lancashire, and being very desirous of avoiding him, Rigby proceeded to Bolton-le-Moor, little imagining that the Royalist army was also counting on taking up its quarters there.

When the Earl of Derby ascertained from the scouts that Rigby had entered Bolton, after raising the siege of Latham House, he urged Prince Rupert to storm the place in revenge of the insults with which Rigby had overwhelmed the Countess for so long a time.

The town was small but well fortified. Rigby had taken into it above 3,000 soldiers, and Colonel Shuttleworth had sent a reinforcement of 1,500 more. The first assault was repulsed with considerable loss. The Parliamentarians massacred in cold blood the soldiers they took on the ramparts. The Prince, hot and haughty of mood, and little accustomed to be resisted, and being also akin to the Countess, was enraged at the insolence of the clowns who had dared

to besiege her in her own house. He yielded readily
to the entreaties of Lord Derby that he would make
a second assault, being quite sure that, if the Royalist
army retired without taking Bolton, the siege of
Latham would soon be renewed.

" Let me have the command of my old soldiers,"
said the Earl, " and give me the charge of the storming
party, and if I do not enter the town, your Highness
will find me in the trench." The Prince hesitated ; the
adventure was a hazardous one to be committed to so
important a man. But Lord Derby insisted, and, after
a terrible struggle of a quarter of an hour, he was the
first to enter the place at the head of his 200 men, and,
possessing himself of a flag carried by an ensign, he
sent it to the Prince, who immediately afterwards
entered the town. They were not able to take Colonel
Rigby, who managed to escape, but 1,600 of his men
were killed on the spot, and 700 taken prisoners.

" On his first passing into the town," says Captain
Halsall, " closely following the foot on their entrance,
his lordship met with Captain Bootle, formerly one of
his own servants, but now the most virulent enemy
against his lady in the siege. Him he did the honour
of too brave a death of dying by his lord's hand, with
some others of his good countrymen who had for
three months thirsted for his lady's and his children's

blood." * The Earl was afterwards bitterly reproached with the death of Bootle.

While Prince Rupert was marching against Liverpool, which he reduced on the 26th of June, the Countess was at length receiving her husband in that house which she had so bravely defended for him and in his name.

With the Earl came Sir Richard Crane, sent by Prince Rupert to present the twenty-two flags taken from the enemy at Bolton to his cousin. A few days before, these very banners had been insolently flourished before her walls. It was with the most profound gratitude to that God in whom she had trusted, that Lady Derby hung them up in the Chapel of Latham, in memory of the deliverance vouchsafed to her.

After the taking of Liverpool, Prince Rupert came to rest for a few days at Latham, among the ruined ramparts and bullet-pierced walls. He was full of admiration at the brave resistance made by a woman against a force so numerous and resolute. He ordered new defences to be made to some of the fortifications, and repairs to others, in order to put the place in a condition to sustain a new siege if necessary. At Lady Derby's request he raised Captain Rawstorne

* HALSALL'S *Siege of Latham House.*

to the post of Governor of the house, with the rank of Colonel, leaving him two squadrons of cavalry. He gave the same rank to Captain Chisenhall, whom he took with him.

Before leaving the Countess the Prince advised her to withdraw to the Isle of Man. He knew the jealousy and suspicion which the power and valour of the Earl excited amongst the courtiers, and, impetuous though he was, he was well aware how doubtful were the chances of war. Lord Derby had re-established order in the little kingdom of Man, and his wife and children would there find security and repose.

" After the siege of Latham . . . the Countess of Derby willingly resigned to her husband the authority which she had never exercised but in his name; and with her children, under the protection of the Earl, retired to the Isle of Man, leaving Latham House to the care of Colonel Rawstorne." * Regardless of the glory and renown she had won, her only desire was to live in peace, far from the troubles which distracted her adopted country. She does not appear to have had much ambition, even for her husband : the remarkable heroism of her character and her conduct was only called forth by duty, and she never seemed to remember her own exploits. Not a word,

* *Postscript to Siege of Latham House.*

not an allusion in her letters ever recalls the fact that
for more than a year, by the exercise of prudence,
resolution, and courage, she had succeeded in keeping
the enemies of her husband and her King in check,
and had finally obliged them to abandon the enterprise
they had so much at heart. She now thought of
nothing but of bringing up her children. " Take great
care of them," the Prince had said. " The children of
such a father and mother will one day render to their
King as much service as yours has received from you."
The services which the Earl of Derby and his wife
rendered to the House of Stuart were not, however,
yet terminated. Charlotte de la Trémoille did not
yet know how much her loyal devotion was to
cost her.

When the Earl of Derby followed the advice of the
Prince and retired to the Isle of Man, with his wife
and his three sons and three daughters, the King had
quitted Oxford, where Essex threatened to besiege
him, and had marched towards the west, where Prince
Rupert, newly entered into York, had attacked the
enemy who had just raised the siege of that city.
They were on Marston Moor. " What post has your
Highness destined for me ?" the Duke of Newcastle
had asked. " I do not count on beginning the action
till to-morrow morning," replied the Prince. " You can

rest till then." But the Duke had scarcely entered his
carriage when the firing began, and hurrying to the
scene of action, he fought as a volunteer. The most
terrible disorder prevailed upon the field. Royalist and ·
Parliamentarian struggled confusedly, without orders
and without generals. The squadrons of Cromwell
alone remained firm, and secured the fortune of the
day. The Cavaliers, misled by the rout of the right
wing of the Parliamentarians, returned from the pursuit
to find the battle-field occupied by a victorious enemy.
Three thousand Royalists were killed ; sixteen hundred
taken prisoners. The standard * of Prince Rupert was
in the hands of the Parliamentarians. He and the
Duke of Newcastle returned to York without speaking
to, without seeing, each other. The next morning the
Prince went to Chester with the remains of his army,
and the Duke embarked for the continent, as the Queen
Henrietta Maria had done two days before. A fortnight after York capitulated.

While the King, eagerly supported by a resolute

---

* " In the middle of this standard was a lion couchant, and behind
him a mastiff biting at him ; from the mastiff's mouth came a streamer,
on which was to be read, ' Kimbolton ;' at its feet were several little
dogs, beneath whose jaws was written, ' Pym, Pym, Pym ;' from the
lion's own jaws proceeded these words, ' Quousque tandem abutere
patientia nostra?' Rushworth, ii. 3, 635. Guizot : Hist. of the
Eng. Revolution.

and numerous party, was fighting Essex in Cornwall, and obliging him to retreat and to submit to a humiliating capitulation, the Parliamentary forces had recommenced the siege of Latham ; but, deprived of the presence of the Countess of Derby, the heroic defence of the place attracted no more attention.   She, who had won the admiration even of her enemies, was in safety in the Isle of Man with her husband and children ; but she had left behind her brave men and well-disciplined soldiers, who for six months more held the house for their lord, displaying a courage and a skill above all praise.

Lady Derby's chaplain, the Rev. S. Rutter, who remained at Latham after her departure, had managed to keep up an active correspondence with her friends in the neighbourhood, and with the King, by means of a woman, who for several months courageously risked her life to take despatches and bring back answers during the frequent sorties made by the besieged.   She was at length taken and put to the torture, but she would reveal nothing, and suffered three fingers on both hands to be burnt off before her tormenters, tired out by her invincible fortitude, at length desisted. Deprived of this faithful messenger they trained a dog to carry the despatches in his collar : they were in cypher, and a friend in the neighbourhood sent them to

those to whom they were addressed. For sever
months the poor animal rendered eminent service, b
at last a soldier, in mere wanton ill temper, fired
musket at him just as he had swum across the moa
and thus their means of communication with the out
world was again lost.

The garrison of Latham had held out since tl
month of July, 1645, hoping for succour from the Kin
But Charles's affairs were looking darker than eve
He had been defeated at Naseby on the 14th of Jun
and had turned towards Scotland to put himself at tl
head of the insurrection raised there by Montrose; b
he was beaten in his attempt to raise the siege
Chester, and forced to retreat to Wales, where h
friends held the country parts. The rising excited l
Montrose had died out like a fire of straw, and tl
heroic adherent of the King had been obliged to hi
himself, and to become, like his master, a wanderer a
a fugitive. The King made it known to the bra
defenders of Latham that he could give them no hel
and that their only course was to surrender. "
melancholy consolation to receive from the master
three kingdoms," says the historian of the House
Stanley; " to see him unable to succour his children
their distress ;—a fatal example of the effects of consta
division in his councils, and of the habitual irresoluti

which prevented this unhappy Prince from being faithful to his best friends."

Hopeless at last, the garrison determined to accept the propositions which had been often addressed to them. The Governor, faithful even in his defeat, stipulated, as the first condition of surrender, the cession to Lady Derby and her children of a third of the revenue of the Earl her husband, with the right to remove all her goods to Knowsley House. He also required that the garrison should be permitted to retire with their arms and baggage, "that all gentle-. men in the house should compound at one year's value for their estates, and that every clergyman should enjoy half the revenue of his living without any oath imposed upon them."* Two of the Parliamentary commanders had already accepted these conditions; the third still stood out, when an Irish soldier, the only traitor in the garrison, swam across the moat, and communicated to the enemy the deplorable state of the besieged,—that they were at the end of their food and ammunition, and unable to hold out any longer. Upon this information, orders were given to surrender the place to the mercy of the Parliament; and the soldiers determining, in spite of the entreaties of the Governor, to hold out no longer, the gates were

* SEACOME'S *House of Stanley.*

opened, the house was pillaged, and the towers and
strong works were razed to the ground. Two or three
little detached buildings alone remained to show where
stood the fortress which had been so long and so
bravely defended.

Amongst the parish documents of Ormskirk are
the receipts for the sale of the planks, beams, and lead
of Latham House, which were all sold by the officers
who destroyed the place.

CHAPTER V.

WE now return to the correspondence of Lady Derby, of which we have lost sight for several years. How deeply interesting would be those lost or stolen letters of hers, particularly any that she might have been able to despatch from Latham by means of the sorties of her brave soldiers, and those that she wrote on her arrival in the Isle of Man. It is not until the date of August, 1646, that we recover possession of these precious documents, which enable us to see into the very household of the Countess, and to be face to face with her anxieties and her joys.

She writes at that time from the Isle of Man in great anxiety. Her son, Lord Strange, of whom we heard nothing during the siege of Latham,—he, as well as his brothers Edward and William, having

8

probably remained with their father,—had secretly quitted the island.

" He stole away from Monsieur his father and from me on the 29th of last month," wrote his mother, "and we know nothing of him since; but we are assured he is in Ireland. The letters he left behind told us he was going to you; and I hope, dear sister, that you will, for my sake, receive him and be a mother to him—all the more because what he has done has offended Monsieur his father and me. If he obeys you, he will the more readily obtain our pardon."

The young Lord Strange was really in Paris, and his mother's next letters are full of thanksgivings to God, who had preserved him, and to her sister-in-law, who had received him and treated him as a mother.

The Duchesse de la Trémoille tried to make his peace with his parents; and Lord Derby thus replied to her on the 21st Dec., 1646 :—

" MADAME,—If my son had committed a much greater fault, I would at your request have forgiven him at once; but having now only forestalled my long-cherished wish that he should have the honour of being with you, I consider him most fortunate in having gained that end. And if, by obeying you as he would myself, he can in any measure merit the honour of your good opinion and friendship, he will gain not only my pardon but my increased affection. This alone can gratify me. It has given me so much happiness to see how you have been pleased to receive him, and what especial care you have deigned to take of him, that I can never offer you sufficiently worthy and humble thanks for it. But if God ever restores to me the power of requiting these deep obligations, you will never, Madame, have a more faithful servant than myself, to whom nothing will be difficult by which I can render you humble service, and prove to you with what devotion

" I am, Madame,

" Your very humble and very obedient brother and servant,

" DERBY."

The Earl consoled himself more readily than he had done of old for the absence of his son, for the affairs of the Royalists were now in a desperate condition. Sir Ralph Hopton and Lord Astley, the last who had held out, had been forced to surrender, and the King had just taken refuge at Keltham, the headquarters of the Scotch, accompanied by M. de Montreuil, the French Envoy, seeking protection from that

people whom in former times his fathers had often led
against England.

The distress of the Royalists was very great.
" You will know as soon as we what the Scotch have
done with the King," wrote Lady Derby to her sister-
in-law in a letter in cypher. " What the Queen is
doing in France is very hurtful to us ; but she cares
neither for what she says nor does, provided she can
recover her position. I hope the gentlemen of the
States will instruct their ambassador to assist me if I
go to London. You will know what my movements
are by what the Scotch do with the King. If they
make me write to my son to contract a marriage that
is unworthy of him, I beg that he will excuse himself
on the ground that he is not thinking of such a thing
at his present age, nor of anything so much as seeing
the world."

The times had indeed become momentous, and the
journey of the Countess proved to be most important.

In the propositions submitted to the King by the
Parliament, which he had just received at Newcastle,
the Earl of Derby found in the list of names excluded
from the amnesty his own, standing next to those of
Prince Rupert and Prince Maurice.* The list con-
sisted of thirty-six persons, of whom the Parliament

* THURLOE'S *State Papers.*

reserved to themselves the power of condemning seven to death.

The King had not yet accepted these conditions, nor did he ever definitively do so; for such acceptance would have implied the adoption of the Covenant, the abolition of the English Church, and the abdication of his power into the hands of the Parliament.

This evidence of animosity towards her husband greatly alarmed Lady Derby, and she resolved to go to London, and do her utmost to get his name erased from the fatal list.

On the 6th of February, 1647, we find her in England, and on the point of starting for London. She writes:—"Trioche" (the confidential attendant of Lord Strange, and much employed by Lady Derby,) " met me in England, and is ready to set out for London, where I wish to be as soon as possible, starting, please God, on Monday. I have been in this part of the country, near one of our houses, for a fortnight, in order to get money for my journey. Many of my friends encourage me to hope; others cause me to fear. I am much troubled by all this doubt and suspense, but God will not forsake me. I will not fail to let you know what happens to me, and I will send Trioche back to you. I have told Monsieur your brother of his arrival. I have left him and his children

very well, but anxious about my voyage. We were
forty-eight hours on the sea, in a very bad boat, and
in great danger. But if God blesses my sufferings,
as I have prayed Him to do, I shall bear everything
well."

On the 10th of March she writes from Chelsea :—
"Immediately after my arrival in Lancashire" (she
spells it *Lenguicher*) "I did myself the honour of
writing to you, and I intended to do the same on
coming here, but could not; for, besides the fatigue
consequent on my journey, the day after my arrival
I received the bad news of the death of Monsieur le
Prince d'Orange,* which distressed me greatly, much
more than all my own sad affairs. They say he died
a most pious and Christian death ; a great consolation
to all who loved him. But you will know more particulars of it than I, who am new to this great world,
where I find everything so changed. I must own
to you, however, that several people who knew me
formerly still show me much affection, and promise
to help me. They advise me not to be impatient; but,
when it is time, to begin by a request to the House of
Peers that the name of Monsieur your brother-in-law
may be taken from the list of those who are not to

* Frederic Henri, third son of William the Silent, uncle of the
Countess of Derby.

hope for pardon. Many say they will help me, and I believe it will be less difficult to obtain this aid from the nobles than from the Commons, who are so much more numerous. I daresay it will be done without much trouble, and God will give me wisdom and prudence.

" The King goes on refusing to do what the Parliament require, and will not hear their ministers preach. He is carefully guarded, and seen by very few. May God counsel him for His glory, and give us a safe peace !

" I have done nothing yet in our own business. Our friends advise me to take no steps till the propositions of peace are again presented to the King, which will not be till the coming of the deputies from Scotland. At present I do not know what to hope. I wish I had your cleverness ; but, besides never having had anything like it, the life I have led since I came to England has been so different from that I am now entering upon, that if God does not give me His powerful help, I know not what I shall do."

By the 25th of March, 1647, the Scotch had betrayed the King into the hands of the Parliament. He had been for a month at Holmby House, in the county of Northampton. The Scotch army had slowly retired, carrying off their 200,000*l.*, the price of their treachery,

but humbled and discontented,—angry with the King,
who would not accept the Covenant, and with the
Parliament of England, for having made them degrade
themselves in their own eyes.

In addition to the anxiety caused by her husband's
affairs, the Countess had now that of a law-suit,
instituted for the recovery of the estate of her brother
the Comte de Laval, who had recently died. His
effects were claimed by Miss Orpe, who maintained
that he had privately married her ; and, to the indignation of Lady Derby, this lady's cause was openly
countenanced by the Queen.

" I can assure you that the Queen of England has
never seen this woman in my house," writes the
Countess to her sister-in-law ; "she has never entered
it except one morning, and when no one was there.
When the Queen has spoken to me about her, I have
always said that I did not believe in any marriage,
and that even if there had been such a thing, a
clandestine marriage was never held good. Her
Majesty does not remember how by her own authority
she annulled a marriage that had been contracted by
the sister of La Harpe, and one of the nephews of
her nurse, and how she threatened an Irish priest with
hanging for having officiated in such an affair."

This nurse of Queen Henrietta Maria had doubtless great influence with her mistress, for it was the circumstance of the marriage of Miss Orpe's brother with one of the daughters of this woman that procured her the royal protection, which, however, was less efficacious in France than in England, for there she could not threaten to hang the judges.

When we see such results from the possession of absolute power, which has fallen into blundering and unscrupulous hands, we can understand how an indignant and outraged nation rises at last into actual rebellion.

"It is with great astonishment that I have read the proceedings of the Queen of England in connection with our law-suit," said the Countess in another letter; "by what I can see, she has done more harm to herself than to us, and every one is ashamed of her. The Electoral Prince came to see me to-day, and I could not help telling him what I thought of the conduct of Prince Rupert in this matter."

Notwithstanding these powerful protectors, Miss Orpe was non-suited, and the property of the Comte de Laval was divided, though not without difficulty, between his brother and sister.

Public affairs now wore a new aspect, but one more troubled and confused than ever. The Parliament, for the time masters of the King, and dread-ing the growing influence of the generals, had voted the disbanding of the army, with the exception of the forces required for the war in Ireland, and for the safety of the garrisons; but neither the independent party, who derived their strength from the army, nor their able leader, who was beginning to exercise a preponderating authority, would permit this.

From his place in Parliament, Cromwell urged the army to resist, and the Countess of Derby thus relates to her sister-in-law the result of his machinations :—

" The army has refused to be disbanded. Yesterday was the day they were to have begun by disbanding the General's regiment" (Fairfax was not to take part in the war in Ireland). " The Parliament sent their Commissioners to the head-quarters of the regiment, but they found no one there, and all the army is assembled. They have chosen two men on whom they can most rely, from every company, and formed them into a sort of council; those of the officers who have refused to do what they want have been disbanded. The General approves of this, and has sent a letter of excuse to the Commissioners for not meeting them. They have applied to Parliament for permission to return, and have returned. God

knows what will come of it! I pray that it may be
for His glory; but I greatly fear the nation is not at
the end of its misery. However, we have the consolation of knowing that things cannot be worse.

"In times like these one cannot think much of one's
own individual troubles, but I am continually assured
that, with God's help, our affairs will come right."

On the 2nd of June, when Lady Derby wrote
thus to her sister-in-law, Cornet Joyce, in the name of
the army, removed the King from Holmby House,
and conveyed him to Newark.

The King in the hands of the army! The blow
was a terrible one for the Presbyterian party, who
saw themselves outflanked by a new power, more
resolute and indomitable than themselves.

"Within a month," writes Lady Derby, on the
21st of June, 1647, to the Duchesse de la Trémoille,
"the face of things here is completely changed. It is
almost beyond conception. The people are so much
excited against the present Government, and show it
so freely at the doors of both Houses of Parliament,
that many of the members are in great danger; and
although the guard has been doubled, that does not
protect them from injury, for those who are brought
there for their protection mock and urge on the others.

"It is said that the approach of the army to London

has occasioned great confusion and alarm, and many
have hastily left the city, believing that there will be
war.   The generals are already chosen " (Massey,
Waller, and Hollis), " but the city of London does not
side with the Parliament.   It desires that the army
should be satisfied, but has hitherto prevented any
warlike resolution.   Each one speaks differently concerning its intentions ; but it is thought the City will
bring the King back, and have the honour of that, and
of making a good peace, in which no distinctions of
party will be recognized.   I hope it may please God
that the arrangement of our affairs should be compre-
hended in this peace, and that He will direct everything for His own glory.

" I have had letters from the Isle of Man, and
everybody there seems very pleased, even those most
employed in public affairs, which are more uncertain
than ever.   I consider my son very fortunate in having
the honour of being with you.

" I have no power of attorney from Monsieur his
father, only a letter in which he tells me that whatever
I may do for his submission to Parliament he will
subscribe to, and other similar things that have no
relation to our affairs in France.

" The King continues with the army ; and the
frequent changes ordered by the Parliament in his

residence—now to one place, now to another—are only attended to by the army as it suits them. They profess that they will respect his person, and they allow him to have his servants and chaplains. The Duke of Richmond sleeps in his bed-room. The Parliament storms against both, but nevertheless gives great support to the orders of the army, which they call *theirs*. They have effaced from their registers all those resolutions against the army which declare they will restore the King and his house to their rights; they promise to maintain the rights of the Parliament and the liberty of the subject; and they say they do not desire the ruin of the King's party. One result of this is that the Lords have already struck out Monsieur your brother-in-law's name from the list of exceptions; and to-day they are doing the same by others. It passed without any opposition, but the Commons have done nothing, as it has not been sent to them yet from the Lords; but I am encouraged to hope that, with God's help, there will be no difficulty.

"I suppose you have already heard how eleven members of the House of Commons have been accused by the army; and the Parliament, in accordance with their desire, have expelled them the House. This change is incredible, for these men" (Hollis, Stapleton, Maynard, &c.,) "were the most distinguished, and

those who led everything; but the alterations in the
Parliament are so extraordinary that if I had not seen
and heard for myself no one could have persuaded me
of them. They are now treated with scorn and hatred,
and every day they are so much insulted in their houses
and their persons that their guard has been doubled.
It is beyond my power to tell what will come of all
this, but I am sure the army will not be disbanded
till everything is settled, and this Parliament ended
and another called. This is all that can be said."

The hopes of the Countess with regard to the
good-will of the army, though destined to be so cruelly
disappointed, were nevertheless not without foundation.
"Some of the leaders, Cromwell and Ireton especially," says M. Guizot, "too clear-sighted to flatter
themselves that their struggle with the Presbyterians
was ended and their victory certain, were uneasy about
the future. They calculated all the chances, and,
seeking to bring matters to a crisis, bethought them if
the favour of the King, raised again by their means,
would not be the best guarantee for the safety of their
party; for themselves the surest means of gaining
fortune and power."

" The King is still fifteen miles from this" (at
Eversham), writes Lady Derby. " The Princes and
Princesses, his children, went from here yesterday to

visit him, and are not to return till to-morrow. Permission for this meeting was asked from the Parliament by Sir Thomas Fairfax, though they had declared any one who should dare to make such a request the enemy of the public. There are various opinions about his intellect, but no doubt about his courage, and that he is a man of his word. In this matter he acted with the army, which has hitherto made the Parliament do what it likes. . . . . It is said by some that the design of the army is to put away all those who hold opinions contrary to their own, and to be governed by the remainder of the Parliament. The King is allowed every kind of liberty; the ambassadors see him and talk to him as formerly. He has received a visit from the Electoral Prince. Before he was in the hands of the army it was a crime to think of anything of the kind.

" Yesterday, the Parliament passed an Act confirming the appointment of Sir Thomas Fairfax to the post of General, which augmentation of rank gives him power over all the forces in the kingdom. Hitherto, he has had the command only of the army that he happened to be with in person ; and now he will have the disposition of all the garrisons, the greater number of which have been already under his control. . . .

" The King showed great delight at the sight of the
Princes his children ; and there was much tenderness
on all sides.   The little Princess " (Elizabeth) " paid
a very apropos compliment to the General, whom she
saw quite unexpectedly, and gave evidence of a great
deal of cleverness,—which they all have, particularly
the youngest " (the Duke of Gloucester).

Lady Derby's stay in London was prolonged ; but
her business did not advance.   She was deeply grieved
at the loneliness and inaction to which her husband
had been condemned for two years.   It was doubtless
at this time that he wrote for his son a series of very
curious instructions for the government of the little
kingdom of Man.   " This island," writes the Earl,
" was sometimes governed by kings, natives of its
own, who were converted to Christianity by St.
Patrick, the Apostle of Ireland.   And Sir John
Stanley, the first possessor of it of that family, was by
his patent styled King of Man, as were his successors
after him, to the time of Thomas, second Earl of
Derby, who, for great and wise reasons, thought fit to
forbear that title.

" And no subject I know hath so great a royalty
as this.   And lest it should at any time be thought
too great, keep this rule, and you will more securely
keep it, ' Fear God and honour the King.'

" When I go to the top of Mount Baroule, by turning myself round, I can see England, Scotland, Ireland, and Wales; and think it a pity to see so many kingdoms at once, which is a prospect no place, as I conceive, in any nation that we know under heaven can afford, and have so little profit from all or any of them.

" But having duly considered thereof, I have, as I think, discovered the reason of it. The country is, indeed, better than I was informed of; for which I blame myself that I enquired so little of it; for, indeed, he who seeks not to know his own is unworthy of what he hath. And I am of opinion this island will never flourish until some trade or manufacture be established in it. But, though you invite strangers or natives to become merchants, yet never anything will be done to the purpose until you yourself lead the way, and by your example and encouragement set this people a pattern.

" By this, or such like means, no doubt but you may grow rich yourself, and others under you improve the land, and set the people to work, so that in time you shall have no beggars nor no loiterers; and where you have one soul now you shall have many; every house will become a little town, and every town a little city; the sea will abound with ships, and the country with people, to the great enrichment of the whole." *

To these wise practical counsels the Earl of Derby added directions for the moral progress of the population.

" Choose for your Bishop," he writes, " a reverend and holy man, who may carefully see the whole clergy do their duty ; but not any person already beneficed in England ; and oblige him you choose to residence. In a few years, the leases will be all expired, and then the bishopric will be worth having ; and, considering the cheapness of the place, I know few bishops in England that can live better than he, the whole being entire, and your prerogative herein very great, to which have a particular regard. . . .

" And if you, even as I designed, set up an university, it may oblige the nations round about us, get friends to the country, and enrich the land, which, in time, will bring something to the lord's purse. And, as the place is cheap, yet well furnished with proper subsistence, and the temptations to idleness or luxury few, education might be had here on the easiest terms. But of this I will tell you more when, please God, I can see you and myself in peace." *

While the Earl was preparing these thoughtful and

* Seacome's *House of Stanley.*

wise directions for the life-long conduct of his son, the loneliness in which the absence of his wife left him was growing more and more oppressive.

In the month of September, 1647, the Parliament at length accorded to Lord Derby's children what they had at first conceded for their personal maintenance, that is, a fifth of their father's revenue. It was only after two years' application that this bounty was assigned to them on the hereditary manor of Knowsley. Catherine and Amelia Stanley were at once sent there by their father, who kept with him only Lady Mary and his sons Edward and William.

A letter from Fairfax to Major Jackson, who was established with his family in the house, had given instructions for the evacuation of the place, and directions had also been conveyed to the keepers to watch that the said Major Jackson destroyed nothing in the house or park before leaving—an injunction which seems to indicate ill will on the part of the Major.

The Countess of Derby was still in London, engaged in her great business. Writing on the 14th of March, 1648, she says :—" I am advised to go to Lancashire, and try to live on what they have allowed my children, for I receive no money ; and I hope my presence may facilitate the means employed for getting

it. Being near, and on the spot, we must live econo-
mically, and make the best of what we have."

In the same letter she gives a very curious picture
of the confusion that prevailed in England on religious
questions. " As for my husband and myself," she
writes, "all that relates to religion is, thank God, so
thoroughly engraved on our hearts, that nothing, with
His grace, can take it away. If the Parliament had
for their end religion and the glory of God, as you
think they have, they would not act with the cruelty
and injustice which characterize all they do. As for
religion, they have so deceived the people that now,
when they perceive their errors, and groan under the
burden of their tyranny, even those who have been
the most attached to their cause deplore our misery
and their own. They would find it hard to tell you
their creed, where there are as many religions as
families. The test is publicly maintained; books
printed which deny the Holy Ghost,—and the persons
known to have produced them not punished; the com-
mandments of God and the confession of faith disregarded; the Lord's prayer neglected, and not thought
necessary to be said; the sacraments administered
according to the fancy of the person administering;
the ministry neglected,—every one who thinks he is
able to preach, even women, may do so without any

examination; baptism is thought nothing of, and not administered to children; and worse things, which make all who have any religion left shudder to see it so abused. As for people who wish ill to us, there are some, but not more than the Lords have who are in Parliament; for the Commons intend to recognize no more aristocrats, but to have perfect equality, only they do not know how to get it managed. If you could hear the discontent amongst them, you would hardly believe it. I speak of those who have risked all for the Parliament, and are the greatest enemies of the King's party. This discontent has reached such a height, that if the Scotch come, as it is supposed they may, there will be very few who will not join them. In consequence of this, all the governors who had been most zealous in the cause of the Parliament have been changed, and replaced by men who regard nothing but their party. But although the Parliament has passed this resolution, if the army disapproves, they must change it : thus one day undoes what the previous one has done. Those only who see what goes on can believe it; and if I myself had not been present, no one could have persuaded me of it.

" If I had the honour of talking to you for a couple of hours, you would soon be convinced of the truth, and

would deplore the sufferings of the Protestant religion
and the profit that the Catholics derive from them.
I have no doubt the Queen will do what she can for
her religion, but I think she ought to consider that she
cannot advance it.   She is most unfortunate ; her own
party are much dissatisfied with her, and say she has
ruined them.   They are no better pleased with the
King."

The tragical end of the drama was approaching;
all the hopes of the Royalists were about to be crushed
by a single blow.   The King had spent two months
and a half at Hampton Court, at first with his court
around him, and freely visited by his children and
friends.   " I saw the King yesterday, for the second
time since it has been permitted to visit him," wrote
Lady Derby, in September, 1647.   " He is hopeful
about his affairs.   The Princes, his children, see him
two or three times a week ; they are living only
three miles from Hampton Court, the finest of his
houses."

Cromwell and Ireton negotiated with the King,
to the suppressed wrath of the Independent party.
Charles multiplied offers ; but, with his incurable
duplicity, at the same time negotiated with Scotland,
where they still hoped to make him accept the Covenant.   In a letter to the Queen, which was seized by

Cromwell, he wrote :—" For the rest, I alone understand my position. Be quite easy as to the concessions I may grant. When the time comes, I shall very
well know how to treat these rogues ; and instead of a
silken garter, I will fit them with a hempen halter."
He added, that he thought he would rather treat with
the Scotch Presbyterians than with the army.

Cromwell and Ireton at once decided on the course
they would take ; and from that time the King's cause
was lost, and his life doomed.

Notwithstanding the hopes he built on his secret
manœuvres Charles was alarmed at the changes that
were being made about him. His faithful counsellors
had been ordered to leave him ; his servants even had
been withdrawn from him, and his guards doubled.
Warnings of assassination reached him every day. He
made up his mind, and on the 11th of November
escaped from his guards and went to the Isle of
Wight, where he was received (not without difficulty)
by the Governor, Colonel Hammond. The King
thought he was safe, and began to negotiate openly
with the Parliament, who sent Commissioners to him ;
and secretly with the Scotch, who promised him an
army ; and even with the leaders of the Independent
party, who were uneasy at the Republican tendencies
manifested by the soldiers.

Charles alone held the thread of all these intrigues, ready at any time to take refuge on the continent if there was really danger.

" I wish to finish with the Scotch before quitting the kingdom," said he : "if they saw me out of the hands of the army they would get more exacting."

He concluded his treaty with the Scotch ; refused the propositions of the Parliament, and sent back their Commissioners.   His escape was planned for the following night, when suddenly the servants were all sent away from the island, the doors of the castle closed, and the guard doubled. Charles Stuart was a prisoner : and in Parliament they ventured to speak of a Republic.

Charles had lost his liberty, but the report of his imprisonment raised him up new defenders.   There were numerous insurrections in the West as well as in the North ; and on the 8th of July the Scotch army, faithful to the treaty of the Isle of Wight, entered England under the orders of the Duke of Hamilton. The Republican chieftains, in spite of the distrust with which Cromwell inspired them, felt that he, and he only, could meet the danger. He hurried to the North, fought the English insurgents under the command of Langdale on the 17th of August, then, uniting with Lambert, he came up with the Scotch at Wigan on the 18th, cut the rear-guard in pieces, and, continuing to advance, . won a last victory at Warrington. The Scotch infantry surrendered, and Hamilton was taken prisoner as he was trying to escape with the cavalry. Every sign of invasion had disappeared, but Cromwell entered Scotland to take from the royalist Presbyterians all means of action and their last hope of safety. Three months later he returned in triumph to head-quarters; and the King, carried off on the 29th of November from Newport, where the Parliament had guaranteed his safety, was shut up in Hurst Castle by order of the army, in an apartment so dark that torches were required at midday, and under the guard of Colonel Ewers, a fierce and ill-mannered gaoler.

While the unhappy King, with the courage and grave dignity which characterized him in his troubles, was passing through all the tragic stages that led to the final sacrifice, his friends and partisans were paying the price of their devotion to him and his cause.

The Countess of Derby had returned to her husband. " Necessity obliges me to quit this place," she writes to her sister-in-law on the 25th of March, 1648, " and our friends of the Parliament advise me to do it, telling me there is no doubt our business will go on very well. There is a gentleman in the same circumstances as ourselves who has been allowed to treat for his estate after having presented his petition, and they have taxed him so high that he will not consent to pay the money. But I am advised to do nothing; there is so much general discontent that those who are in office say in confidence things cannot be long without change."

CHAPTER VI.

LETTERS AFTER THE KING'S DEATH.

FIFTEEN months passed, and what changes had taken place! There was not a word from the Countess of Derby to her sister-in-law during that terrible period. She may not have written, or her letters may have been lost. The King's trial, his death, and the first months of the Republic, remain shrouded in melancholy silence. One cry of indignation alone comes from the Isle of Man, and it is from the Earl of Derby.

The Parliament had again tried to shake his fidelity. The King he had served was dead; and Ireton wrote to induce him to surrender the Isle of Man to the Parliament, promising him the free enjoyment of all the rest of his possessions in return. Here is the reply made by the Earl :—

"Castletown, July 22nd, 1649.

"SIR,—I received your letter with indignation and scorn, and return you this answer : That I cannot but wonder whence you should gather any hopes from me, that I should, like you, prove treacherous to my sovereign, since you cannot but be sensible of my actings in his late Majesty's service ; from which principles of loyalty I am no whit departed. I scorn your proffers, disdain your favour, and abhor your treason ; and am so far from delivering up this island to your advantage, that I will keep it to the utmost of my power to your destruction. Take this for your final answer, and forbear any further solicitations ; for, if you trouble me with any more messages on this occasion, I will burn the paper and hang the bearer. This is the immutable resolution, and shall be the undoubted practice of him, who accounts it his chiefest glory to be

"His Majesty's most loyal and

"obedient servant,

"DERBY."

At the same time that the Earl sent this haughty reply to General Ireton, he published in London a declaration, consisting of several pages, expressing the same resolution, and ending with this paragraph :—

"And I do hereby declare, that, to the utmost of

my power, I shall faithfully endeavour to hold out this island to the advantage of his Majesty, and the annoyance of all rebels and their abettors, and do cheerfully invite all my allies, friends, and acquaintance, all my tenants in the counties of Lancaster and Chester, or elsewhere, and all other his Majesty's faithful and loyal subjects, to repair to this island, as their general rendezvous and safe harbour, where they shall receive entertainment, and such encouragement as their several qualities and condition shall require; where we will unanimously employ our forces to the utter ruin of these unmatchable and rebellious regicides, and the final destruction of their interests both by land and sea.   Neither shall any apprehension of danger either to my life or estate appal me; but I shall on all occasions (by God's assistance) shew myself ready to express my duty and loyalty with hazard of both; and this I shall adventure for the future with more alacrity, for as much as, in all my former actings in his Majesty's service, I never did any thing with relation to the trust reposed in me, that awakens my conscience to repentance.

" DERBY."

" From Castletown, in the Isle of Man,
"July the 18th, 1849." *

* State Trials.

On the 27th July, 1649, two months after this
declaration of war, the Countess of Derby wrote to
her sister-in-law :—" I believed, as you did, that our
business was accomplished, and the person who
hitherto managed it brought us the news with the
congratulations natural in the circumstances; his stay
here was only for a few days, but when he got back to
England he found everything in worse condition than
ever, and some of our estates already given away—a
thing which has never yet been done. No reason was
given for this alteration, but I know it was occasioned
by petitions, full of false representations, having been
presented to Parliament by low people, and, although
numbers know and say how false are these statements,
they will not hear reason. Dear sister, if you had the
least notion of the truth, you would change your
opinion. The sects of which you speak increase daily,
and it makes one's hair stand on end to think of it.
The Koran is printed with permission. It is common
to deny both God and Jesus Christ, and to believe
only in the Spirit of the Universe. I am not repeating
from report, I have heard these blasphemies; as for
baptism, they make a joke of it. I assure you, the
hearts of those who have any religion left bleed to talk
of these things.

  " They threaten this poor place ; but we will do

our utmost, with the grace of God, to defend it.   He
knows how my husband and I have always sought
His glory rather than our own interests, and that we
have loved the religion I profess above all others.

"How great a consolation it would be if I could
tell you what is in my mind, for I am sure you would
pity us, and our sufferings would grieve you, and make
you hate the malice of our enemies, and those of God
and true religion.   God will not abandon His Church.
The Gospel does not promise temporal blessings as
signs of the good cause.   It is by tribulation and
misery that we are to come to heaven.   I prepare
myself for it with joy diminished only by the thought
of my poor children and their father.   But I hope God
will help them, and that those to whom they have the
honour of belonging will not suffer them to perish ;
and that, since they cannot help them against their
enemies, they will at least have pity on their misery.
Dear sister, forgive the terrors of an afflicted mother,
who opens her heavy heart to you, and begs you, in
God's name, to give her your help."   (Then in cypher):
—"The only cause of their ill will to us is their desire
to have this island, and, when they have got us into
their power, to take our lives and our property.   My
wish is to be protected by some foreign state or prince.
But we must implore your aid and advice in the

extreme distress in which our poor family is placed. . .
The person who brought us the news of our composition, also brought a passport for my husband to return
to England ; but if he used it his life would be in
danger. You may judge by this with what kind of
people we have to do, and of the integrity of their
intentions."

So much trouble told upon Lady Derby's health.
She was ill when she wrote the letter we have just read.
A few lines only on the 15th of October show that she
was worse.   On the 30th of December she wrote :—

" For seven weeks I have scarcely taken sleep or
nourishment, and I believed God, in His mercy, had
made me satisfied to quit this world, having given me
the firm assurance of the pardon of my sins through
the merits of His son, and perfect confidence in my
salvation and in the joys of a future state. But it
has pleased Him to keep me longer in this miserable
world ; and I hope He will give me grace to employ
for His glory the life to which He has so miraculously
restored me. To have suffered in so good and holy
a cause gave me great repose of conscience during my
illness ; and I would not exchange the least happiness
I have experienced for all the joy of my persecutors,
since the prosperity of the wicked is only for a time.

" I hope, dear sister, that my letters have shown

you the truth, and the designs they have in England with regard to religion " (the Duchesse de la Trémoille had evidently been led away by the pious protestations of Cromwell) ; " and permit me to say, that nothing has ever so grieved me as to see that you entertained a belief so opposed to what is professed in England and other places where these monsters have power. Not a week passes but some of their people are here ; and to hear the blasphemies they utter is almost beyond belief, and how they pervert the Scriptures, declaring that whatever wickedness is done by the elect, is done by the inspiration of the spirit they call Holy ; and that every one may serve God after his own fashion ; that Christ and His Apostles had some light, but that *they* were come to restore religion, and that there was more error in the Presbytery than in the Church of England under the government of bishops. I declare that what I am writing is the least extravagant of their doctrines, in which one can perceive no foundation, since they change according to their fancy, and, provided nothing is said against their tyrannical Government, every kind of vice the most monstrous, and of heresy the most execrable and unheard of, are endured. I am assured that, if this goes on, in a few years the Catholic religion will be openly professed in England : it is

now very freely tolerated, and the votaries of this
religion live peaceably and enjoy their property.

"I am troubling you too much, dear sister. It is
true, when I am on this topic it is not easy for me to
quit it."

Lady Derby's reflections on the progress of
Catholicism continued to alarm the Duchesse de la
Trémoille ; a letter written by her two months before
only reached the Isle of Man in January, 1650, and the
doubt which she then expressed caused Lady Derby
to write without delay on the 20th of that month :—

"I have read what you were good enough to send
me in cypher about the King's affairs" (Charles II.—
who had been proclaimed in Scotland and Ireland at
the very time that the Parliament had been forced by
Cromwell to proclaim the Republic, and who was still
in Holland) ; "but, if you are not mistaken in the
cypher for my husband, I believe exactly the contrary :
for, by all possible assurances and protestations, you
may rest satisfied, dear sister, that he is as true a Protestant as ever, and that he has not the least inclination to become a Catholic ; and for this I give you my
word. But, dear sister, how much mistaken they are
who tell you there are none such in England. I
received a letter yesterday from a person of credit,
who has always been of their party, who tells me that

one of their ministers, whose name she gave me, and the place where he preached, had said and maintained openly in church that there was no greater divinity than himself, and that, as he was not God, therefore, there could be no God. Some one complained of it to the governor of the town ; but the man was not punished, and nobody seemed to consider it strange. If you understood English, I would send you the letter. One of our people, who returned from Scotland a short time ago, had seen many sorcerers burned, who all declared that they were always present with Cromwell when he fought ; and others in England, near Newcastle, say the same thing, our doctor being present at the time ; and there is a sorcerer now in prison in Edinburgh, who affirms that he was present when Cromwell renounced his baptismal vow."

What a strange medley of faith and superstition, of strength of mind and credulity ! The strict Huguenot and the lady of rank were equally outraged by this burst of mad liberty ; in her alarm and contempt she confounds the Koran, Catholicism, and sorcerers, with levellers, Atheists, and Pantheists. When we find people speaking of the spirit of the universe and the divinity of human nature in the very midst of the Rebellion of 1649, we are tempted to exclaim, " There is nothing new under the sun."

In the midst of the sufferings and anxieties and
the terrible realities with which Lady Derby was surrounded, we are surprised and not a little amused to find
several of her letters filled with questions of etiquette.
On the 1st of May, 1648, the Prince de Tarente had
married Amelie de Hesse Cassel, daughter of the
reigning Grand Duke.   At the congress of Münster,
in 1643, the Duc de la Trémoille put forward pretensions to the crown of Naples, in right of a marriage
contracted in 1521 between François de la Trémoille
and the granddaughter of Frederic III, King of Naples.
Mdlle. de la Trémoille was about to be presented at
court, and there was some question as to her " tabouret."   The mother therefore applies to the aunt for her
reminiscences on this subject ; and, from her retirement
in the Isle of Man, after having lived for twenty-four
years away from France and the court, Charlotte de
la Trémoille throws herself eagerly into the discussion.

She refers for a moment to the subject of her own
" tabouret."   " You were in Paris," she writes to her
sister-in-law, " when the Queen, the King's mother"
(Marie de Medicis) " deprived me of it ; and it was that
very summer, at St. Germains, that she gave it back to
me, saying that she did so with all her heart, for she
believed it was my right.   The Cardinal de Richelieu,
who answered for me, said as much to my mother

when she went to thank him; and I have kept it ever since at the court of both Queens." "Le tabouret," or right of sitting on a stool in presence of royalty, was accorded to Mademoiselle de la Trémoille, to the great satisfaction of her aunt.

On the 2nd of June, 1650, Charles II. embarked for Scotland, fifteen days after the execution of Montrose. To acquire a crown he had accepted the Covenant, and sacrificed his own honour and the life of his servant; his father had refused to the end to preserve his crown at such a price.

"It is said that the King has certainly concluded a treaty with the Scots," writes Lady Derby in May, 1650, "and that he is soon to be in Scotland in person. If this news had been known two days earlier, the life of the Marquis of Montrose might have been saved ; within three days he has been condemned and executed. He was to have been commander in Ireland if it had pleased God to spare his life. I pray that this event may not damp people's spirits."

The King was no sooner landed in Scotland than his faithful servants found all their troubles increased, —a melancholy foretaste of the sacrifices which they were destined to make in his cause.

On the 8th of June, 1650, Lady Derby writes to her sister-in-law :—

"Since my last letter I have received news of your nieces in England which afflicts me not a little; and though I can think of nothing to relieve them, I hope to find some comfort in telling you my troubles, for I know that you will share, and, if possible, remedy them. More than two years ago, when I was in England, and intending to come here, I was advised, with some show of reason, to send for your two nieces, Catherine and Amelie, and to leave them at Knowsley during my absence, that they might keep possession of the house, and receive the income granted to the children of delinquents, for so they call us" (the petition putting forward a claim to this revenue is drawn up in the name of the six children of the Earl of Derby), "and which was the fifth part of the revenue of their father's estates. Before I sent for them from this place, I procured passports from the Parliament and the General" (Sir Thomas Fairfax), "and his protection for my daughters, and they have been there two whole years without any one ever having disturbed either them or their people. But about three weeks ago, a man of the name of Birch, the governor of a small town called Liverpool, took them prisoners, and confined them in the said town, where they are now in custody with their attendants. No reason is given for this, but we hear it is because they are thought to be too much liked, and that people were beginning to make applications to the Parliament in the hope that their father might come to terms, of which I see no chance. They are kept so strictly that no one about them is allowed to go to the distance of even six miles from their residence without permission, running the risk of being shot like a criminal.

" They persecute those who belonged to their own party before this horrible attempt against the King, quite as much as those of his party. In all this we acknowledge the righteous judgments of God. Here is all I can tell you, dear sister, on this unhappy subject. I trust in God that He will protect them, and I do not doubt that He will. We hear that they are bearing it bravely, and I have no doubt this is true of the eldest ; but my daughter Amelie is delicate and timid, and is undergoing medical treatment, by order of M. de Mayerne.* They are in a wretched place, ill lodged, and in a bad air; but these barbarians think of nothing but carrying out their damnable designs, which could not be worse if all hell itself had invented them."

Bradshaw's hatred of the Earl of Derby had conceived this method of satisfaction ; it was easy enough

* A medical man in whom Lady Derby placed great confidence.

to understand the end he had in view in thus perse-
cuting the Earl's children.

Their sufferings continued to increase; the income
allowed them by Parliament was not sufficient even to
procure them bread; and if it had not been for the
liberality of the poor impoverished Royalists, and the
fidelity of their own servants, who went about begging
for them from house to house, these poor girls, Lady
Catherine and Lady Amelia Stanley, would have died
of hunger. At length they applied to Fairfax, who
had always been kind to them; and he wrote to the
Earl of Derby to this effect, " That if his lordship
would deliver the Isle of Man to the Parliament's
commands, his children should not only be set at
liberty, but he should peaceably return to England,
and enjoy one moiety of all his estate." *

This was more than Lord Derby had reason to
expect from the Parliament; yet the Isle of Man was
the brightest jewel in his coronet; a safe and peaceful
retreat in stormy times; and a place where the authority of the King and the Church was still recognized.
He replied to Sir T. Fairfax:—

" I am deeply afflicted for the sufferings of my
children. It is not the course of great and noble minds
to punish innocent children for their father's offences.

* SEACOME'S *House of Stanley*.

It would be a clemency in Sir Thomas Fairfax either to send them back to me, or to Holland or to France ; but if he can do none of these, my children must submit to the mercy of God Almighty, but shall never be redeemed by my disloyalty." *

In addition to her anxiety for her daughters, the Countess of Derby had other troubles. Her son, Lord Strange, had left France, and to her great grief was living in idleness in Holland.

"We have written to your nephew, desiring him to return to France," she writes to her sister-in-law, "that he may see a campaign there ; for it is shameful for a person of his age" (he was under twenty-three,) "never yet to have seen anything; he has received some hints of this kind from those about him which have piqued him greatly, and inspired him with a desire to see service, for which I do not blame him."

Young Lord Strange had no very great desire to see service, and other ties kept him in Holland. He had conceived a passionate affection for Mdlle. de Rupa, a young German lady of good family, but without fortune or rank. This new trouble roused in Lady Derby's mind the strongest feelings of anger; her son had often offended her, and in this matter not only were her maternal feelings wounded, but her

* SEACOME'S *House of Stanley.*

family pride, accustomed as she was to great alliances, was outraged. She therefore resolved to go herself to Holland to break off the connection.

Charles II. had been a month in Scotland when she wrote from Kircudbright in August, 1650 :—

"DEAR SISTER,—I had the honour of writing to you two days before my departure from the Isle of Man, which was on the 26th of last month," (this letter is lost,) "when I told you my resolution to go through this country to Holland, to remedy, if possible, this sad business; but finding that the English army had come here in great force, I could not travel without a passport; I have sent to ask for one, and I shall wait for it in the Isle of Man, to which place I return to-day, please God; with a fair wind it is but a ten hours' voyage. I have been here fifteen days, suffering every imaginable inconvenience, being reduced to eat oaten bread, and some of us to lodge in the house of the chief person of the place, though I never saw anything so dirty. But this is nothing to the religion. I fear greatly the result of this war, and I assure you that those who are in power are not so much in favour of monarchy as against the Duke of Hamilton, and his faction. The King behaves with wonderful prudence; he is obliged to listen continually to sermons against

his father, blaming him for all the blood that was
shed ; and those which I have heard in this place are
horrible, having nothing of devotion in them, nor
explaining any point of religion, but being full of
sedition ; naming people by their names, and treating of everything with such ignorance, and without
the least respect or reverence, that I am so scandalised
I do not think I could live with a quiet conscience
among these atheists. I shall do my utmost to make
out my journey from the island ; if my passport comes,
as I have reason to hope it will, I shall certainly
attempt it. But if it does not, look with compassion,
dear sister, on this unfortunate affair, which is of so
much consequence to my poor distressed family ; have
pity on an unfortunate mother, distracted with grief,
for I know not what to do. If my passport is refused,
I see no means of breaking off this affair by personal
interference, unless you would take it in hand, with
that prudence and skill with which you manage whatever you are pleased to undertake."

The passport did not come, and all Lady Derby's
anger could not prevent the marriage of her son with
Mdlle. de Rupa, for which she never forgave him to
the end of her days.

It was no doubt by his wife's advice that the Earl

of Derby, in drawing up his will before his departure
from the Isle of Man, wrote these words :—

"I give and bequeath to my most gracious sovereign
and liege Lord Charles, the second of that name, one
cup of fine gold of the value of one hundred pounds,
humbly beseeching his Majesty, if God shall call me
out of the world before I see my estate settled by his
grace and favour, my chief honour and estate may
descend upon my son Edward and his issue male,
and in default of him upon my son William and his
issue male, or in default of any such issue upon my
daughter Mary and her two sisters Catherine and
Amelia successively ; and this by reason of my just
sense against Charles, my eldest son, for his disobe-
dience to his Majesty in the matter of his marriage,
as his Majesty well knows, and for his going to join
the rebels of England at this time to the great grief
of his parents, by which he hath brought a stain upon
their blood if he were permitted to inherit."

The father spoke harshly when he styled the proceedings of his son an adhesion to the rebels : Charles
Stanley had written to the Duchesse de la Trémoille
in December, 1650 :—

"Some days ago I received letters from the Isle
of Man in which I am desired by my father and
mother to address myself to M. de la Trémoille and

to you, and to receive your orders as if they came
from my parents themselves, a command which I am
very willing to obey. Some people in England have
sent me word that, if my father did not make his peace
with the Parliament within two months, neither he
nor any of his race after him should enjoy his estates
in that country; urging upon me that, since they were
sure the Parliamentarians would never come to terms
with my father, I should do well to go over and make
terms with them on my own account, which being
done, my father might enjoy his property in my
name. I do not wish to say anything about this to
my father and mother until I have your approval
of it. I hope you have not so bad an opinion of
me as to think that in this matter I look to my own
profit so much as to the good of our house; whatever advantage I may reap from this negotiation, my
chief desire is that I may bring back the waters to
their source."

The Duchesse de la Trémoille could scarcely have
advised "this negotiation," entirely opposed as it was
to the wishes and principles both of Lady Derby and
her husband. Yet it seems probable that Lord Strange
disregarded her silence or disapproval, for he certainly
went to England; we find, indeed, no trace of his stay
there, but we may presume that he lived quietly at

Knowsley.   To the last his mother never forgot his
offences.

"I give to my son, Charles, Earl of Derby, the sum
of five pounds," she writes in her will.   She was poor,
no doubt, but even the smallest token of remembrance
would have been less cruel than this bequest, evidently
intended as it was to disinherit him.   Forgiveness
was not one of Lady Derby's virtues.

While her letters were thus filled with indignation
against her son, and especially against "the Delilah," as
she constantly calls her daughter-in-law, who had
drawn him into a marriage so highly disapproved by
all his family, events were hurrying on rapidly in
Scotland.   Cromwell had entered that country on the
22nd of July, 1650, almost at the same moment as the
King, with an army of about fifteen thousand men.
As soon as he had crossed the borders of Scotland he
addressed his army, exhorting them "as Christians and
soldiers, to be doubly and trebly diligent, to be wary
and worthy, for sure enough we have work before us!
But have we not had God's blessing hitherto?   Let us
go on faithfully and hope for the like still."

Cromwell might well be hopeful, for the King,
against whom he had come to fight, was already half
vanquished.   Treated as a prisoner in the country
which had just recalled him, Charles was not even

present at the councils where his affairs were discussed. While surrounding him with all the pomps
of royalty, they never took the trouble of consulting
him.

" The King gains everybody's affection," writes
Lady Derby, "though he is treated very shamefully.
The Church wished to keep him away from the army,
but he presented himself to them, and they received
him with the greatest joy ; the Church, fearing that
he would become too popular, sent him away again.
Cromwell, who is general of the English army, has
sent in a declaration along with that of the Parliament,
and the Church has replied, on its own authority,
without consulting either the King or the Council
of State. The Pope himself never assumed such
authority."

This Church of Scotland, for which Lady Derby
had conceived such an aversion, or rather for the
fanatics in it who were stirring up the people, required
the King to sign a declaration, acknowledging and
deploring the evil deeds of his father, his mother's
idolatries, and the sin which he had himself committed
in treating with the Irish rebels. For the first time
since he entered Scotland, Charles allowed his indignation to appear.

" I could never again look my mother in the face

if I were to sign such a paper," he exclaimed. But they insisted, and the declaration was signed.

Meantime, Cromwell continued his march into Scotland, through a desolated country, the people having retired before him, and destroyed all the crops as they went. Finding neither provisions nor enemies, he withdrew to Dunbar, closely followed by the Scottish army, under command of Sir Alexander Leslie, whom he attacked, and completely defeated there on the 3rd of September, 1650. Six days afterwards he was master of Leith and Edinburgh, the Castle alone holding out against him.

Charles had been taken to Perth, where he heard without regret of the defeat of the fanatics, and the disorganization of the Presbyterian party. On the 1st of January, 1651, he was crowned at Scone, and his position began to look more hopeful. The Royalists were active in England, and the Scotch Parliament was entirely in the hands of the moderate party, who, with Hamilton and Lauderdale at their head, invited the King to assume the command of his army.

While these favourable changes were taking place in the King's affairs, Cromwell fell dangerously ill, and was at one time thought to be dying. But the strength of his constitution and of his will prevailed over the disorder, and in July, 1651, he reappeared at the head of his forces, laying siege to Perth, and threatening to deprive Charles, who was encamped with his army at Stirling, of this the chief seat of his Government.

The King suddenly determined to break up his camp, and to carry the war into England. He believed the Royalists only waited for his appearance to rise in his favour, and that all who were weary of the tyranny of the army would join him, and he counted on his Scotch subjects proving their loyalty by sharing his fortunes. Many of his friends disapproved of this bold measure, but few dared to speak out. Argyle alone tried to dissuade him ; but, having failed, and being too proud to enter England in the train of the Duke of Hamilton, he withdrew from the expedition, and retired to his castle of Inveraig.

On the 31st of July, Charles set out for Carlisle at the head of an army of from twelve to fourteen thousand men, with David Leslie as his Lieutenant-General. Eight days afterwards Cromwell also left Scotland, and advanced in the King's rear.

As soon as Charles set foot in England, he sent for the Earl of Derby. Lady Derby, writing from the Isle of Man on the 1st of September, 1651, says :—

" We are still existing here, by the goodness of God, who has permitted my husband to reach the

King, his master, in safety, with a considerable force.
He took with him ten ships, which nothing but God's
help could have brought here safely; for since his
departure we have been harassed by the enemy's
ships. He left this on Wednesday the 13th of last
month, and landed in England on the 15th, in a part
of Lancashire called Wyrewater. I hear that the King
received him with great joy and with every mark of
affection. I wait impatiently for further particulars,
which I much fear will not arrive soon on account of
the enemy's ships which infest this coast."

Here the letters cease for six months. The
Countess of Derby said little in times of sorrow; the
great epochs of her life are marked by silence.

CHAPTER VII.

THE LAST DAYS OF A NOBLE LIFE.

On the first summons from the King the Earl had left the Isle of Man to join the royal army, Charles assuring him that not only the Royalists but the Presbyterians also had promised to rise in his favour. But on reaching Lancashire with three hundred gentlemen, he found that the King had already passed through that county, and had left Major-General Massey at Warrington to receive him. On the night of his arrival he had an interview with some of the Presbyterian party.

"Gentlemen," said Lord Derby, "I am come to do his Majesty all the service in my power. The King has given me assurance under his own hand" (he showed them the King's letter,) "that you are all disposed to join with him; to that end I am ready to

receive whoever are pleased to come to me, and with
them to march immediately to his Majesty."

To this, one of their ministers, in behalf of himself
and his brethren, replied :—

"We hope that your lordship will put away all the
Papists that you have brought from the Isle of Man,
and that you will take the covenant with us ; after
that we will follow you willingly."

"Sir, I hope this is only your own opinion," said
the Earl; "and therefore I desire that the gentlemen
present will be pleased to deliver their own sentiments."

"His Majesty has taken the covenant," they
replied, "and has thereby given encouragement to
all his subjects to do the same. If your lordship
will not put away all Papists, and enter publicly
into the solemn league and covenant, we cannot
join you."

"Upon these terms I might long since have been
restored to my whole estate, and the blessed martyr
Charles I. to all his kingdom," said Lord Derby. "I
am not now come to dispute, but to fight for his
Majesty's restoration, and will, upon the issue of the
first battle, humbly submit myself to his Majesty's
directions on that point; I will refuse none of any
persuasion whatsoever that come up cheerfully to

serve the King; and I hope you will give me the same freedom and latitude to engage whom I can for his Majesty's preservation; I am well assured that all those gentlemen I have brought with me are sincere and honest friends to his Majesty's person and interest." *

Major Massey seconded Lord Derby with the strongest arguments in his power, but the Presbyterians obstinately insisted on their demands. "The old leaven had taken too much effect, and soured them too far to be sweetened by any arguments or reasonings whatsoever," says the historian of the House of Stanley. Then Lord Derby rose, and ended the conference with these words :—

"Gentlemen, if you will be persuaded to join with me, I make no doubt but in a few days to raise as good an army to follow the King as that he has now with him, and, by God's blessing, to shake off the yoke of bondage resting upon both you and us; if not, I cannot hope to effect much. I may, perhaps, have men enough at my command; but all the arms are in your possession, without which I shall only lead naked men to slaughter. However, I am determined to do what I can, with the handful of gentlemen now with me, for his Majesty's service, and if I perish, I perish;

* SEACOME'S *House of Stanley.*

but if my master suffer, the blood of another Prince, and all the ensuing miseries of this nation, will lie at your doors." He then took horse, accompanied by the gentlemen he had brought with him from the Isle of Man, and some few of the royal party who came in to him.*

Resting for a few days at Preston, he found that the secret warrants which he had caused to be dispersed in all the chief towns of the county were beginning to produce their effect; a number of cavaliers had already joined him, and he was hoping for further reinforcements, when he learned that Colonel Robert Lilburn, despatched by Cromwell to repress the movements by the Royalists in the West, had come to Manchester with a considerable body of troops. Lord Derby had with him only six hundred horse, whom he had had no time to train; he, however, gave orders upon this to march to Wigan, a town devoted to the King, where he hoped to add to his numbers; but before he could reach that place, Lilburn came up with him in a narrow lane, where his cavalry fought at a great disadvantage. The brilliant courage of Lord Derby and his cavaliers was forced to give way before the numbers and the regular discipline of the Republican troops. At the head of his vanguard the

* SEACOME'S *House of Stanley.*

Earl twice forced a passage through the whole body of the enemy. He had two horses killed under him, but was both times remounted by a faithful servant, a Frenchman, who helped him at the peril of his life. At the third charge, after seeing his best friends fall by his side, he fought his way through the fugitives, with six gentlemen of his party, and having reached the town, he leaped from his horse at a door which stood open, and immediately shut it behind him before the enemy could come up. The woman of the house contrived to keep the door locked long enough to give him time to escape by the back, and take refuge with one of his friends. He was found to have received seven shots on his breastplate, fourteen cuts on his helmet, and five or six slight wounds in his arms and shoulders, while his friends were nearly all left dead on the spot.

When his wounds were dressed, Lord Derby procured a disguise, and set out to join the King. Charles had by this time reached Worcester, after having forced a passage across the Mersey in face of Lambert's troops. He had gained very few recruits; only a small number of cavaliers had joined him, and these were scantily attended : though he was received with acclamation by the people, they did not rise in his favour. Religious and national animosity cooled the enthusiasm of the English, whether Catholics or Anglicans, for the cause of a king who came surrounded by Scotchmen and Presbyterians. The Royalists were disliked even by the English Presbyterians, and the Scotch felt that their cause was bad. Leslie himself was grave and dispirited.

" How can you be sad, General," said the King to him as they approached Worcester, " when you are at the head of so brave an army? Do you not think they look well ? "

" Sir," answered Leslie, in his ear, " I am melancholy indeed, for I well know that army, how well soever it looks, will not fight."*

The troops of Lambert and Harrison were scouring the country, and arresting all suspected travellers, when Lord Derby, in disguise, and with only three attendants, left Wigan at nightfall to join the King at Worcester. They dared not keep the high road, but made their way with difficulty from house to house, and from cottage to cottage, lying concealed by day, and travelling during the night. Reaching the borders of Shropshire and Staffordshire, near Newport, he was received by a Royalist family, who directed him to a place of safety, where he might take a few days' rest. His wounds, though not dangerous, were very painful,

* CLARENDON, *History of the Rebellion.*

and he could scarcely keep his seat on horseback when he arrived at the castle of Boscobel, a small country-house belonging to the Giffards, a Catholic family, who themselves lived on their property of Chillington, to which Boscobel was attached. The situation was wild and solitary, on the summit of a hill, and completely surrounded by thick forests. The charge of this place was entrusted to a family of Catholic peasants, the Penderells, whose name became afterwards so well known for their devotion to the person of the fugitive King.

In this refuge, intended for the concealment of proscribed priests, the Earl might hope to defy the pursuit of his enemies ; and here he rested for two days. On the 31st of August, 1651, he continued his journey to Worcester, which he reached on the 2nd of September. The fatal battle of Worcester was fought on the following day, when the Royalists were completely routed by Cromwell, the King scarcely escaping with his life. A little band of Royalists, Lord Derby, Lord Cleveland, and Colonel Wogan, by surrounding and protecting him with their swords, contrived to force a passage for him through the ranks of the enemy, they themselves remaining behind to cover his retreat. At the end of the day, they rejoined him at some distance from the town, and,

Lord Derby advising his concealment at Boscobel, Mr. Charles Giffard, who was present, offered to conduct him thither. Accompanied by his faithful servants, Charles marched all night, and arrived early next morning at the castle of White Ladies, which also belonged to the Giffards. Some hours afterwards he left this house, conducted by William Penderell, to whom Lord Derby had particularly commended him, parting from the friends who had served him so faithfully, in order that he might reach the coast and embark for France.

The perils through which he effected his escape are well known. Some of his followers shared his fortunes; but Lord Derby, attempting, with Lord Lauderdale, to enter Cheshire or Lancashire, fell into the hands of a troop of horse, accompanied by a regiment of foot, commanded by Major Edge, who were marching towards Worcester to join the Parliamentary army. The Earl and his companions, making themselves known, asked for quarter, which was granted on condition that they gave up their arms and surrendered themselves prisoners. Lord Lauderdale was sent to another part of the country, and his life was spared. The Earl of Derby was immediately conducted to Chester, from which place, soon after his arrival, he wrote the following letter to his wife :—

" My dear Heart,—It hath been my misfortune since I left you not to have one line of comfort from you, which hath been most afflictive to me ; and this, and what I now further write you, must be a mass of many things in one.

" I will not stay long on particulars ; but, in short, inform you that the King is dead or narrowly escaped. in disguise, whither is not yet known ; all the nobles of the party killed or taken, save a few ; and it matters not much where they be. The common soldiers are dispersed, some in prison, some sent to other nations, and none like to serve any more on the same score. I escaped a great danger at Wigan ; but met with a worse at Worcester, being not so fortunate as to meet with any that would kill me, and thereby have put me out of the reach of envy and malice. Lord Lauderdale and I, having escaped, hired horses, and, falling into the enemy's hands, were not thought worth killing ; but had quarter given us by one Captain Edge, a Lancashire man, and one that was so civil to me, that I and all that love me are beholding to him.

" I thought myself happy in being sent prisoner to Chester, where I might have the comfort of seeing my two daughters, and to find means of sending to you ; but I fear my coming here may cost me dear, unless Almighty God, in whom I trust, will please to help me

some other way. But whatsoever come of me, I have
peace in my own breast, and no discomfort at all but
the afflictive sense I have of your grief and that of my
poor children.

" Colonel Duckenfeld, Governor of this town, is
going, according to his orders from the Parliament,
General to the Isle of Man, where he will make known
unto you his business.

" I have considered your condition and my own,
and thereupon give you this advice. Take it not as
from a prisoner, for, if I am never so close confined,
my heart is my own, free still as the best, and I scorn
to be compelled to your prejudice, though by the
severest tortures. I have procured Baggerley, who
was prisoner in this town, to come over to you with
my letter. I have told him my reasons, and he will
tell them to you ; which done, may save the spilling
of blood in that island, and it may be of some here,
dear to you. But of that take no care ; neither treat at
all, for I perceive it will do you more hurt than good.

" Have a care, my dear soul, of yourself, and of
my dear Mall, Ned, and Billy ; as for those here, I
will give them the best advice I can. It is not with
us as heretofore. My son,* with his spouse, and my

---

* Lord Strange, who, as we have seen, had come some time
before to England, in spite of all his mother's efforts to prevent it.

nephew Stanley have come to see me. Of them all, I will say nothing at this time, excepting that my son shows great affection, and is gone to London with exceeding concern and passion for my good. He is changed much for the better, I thank God, and would have been a greater comfort to me if I could have left him more, or if he had provided better for himself.

" The discourse I have had here of the Isle of Man has produced the enclosed, or at least such. desires of mine as I hope Baggerley will deliver to you upon oath to be mine ; and truly, as matters go, it will be best for you to make condition for yourself, children, and friends, in the manner as we have proposed, or as you can further agree with Colonel Duckenfeld, who being so much a gentleman born, will doubtless, for his own honour, deal fairly with you.

" You know how much that place is my darling ; but since it is God's will to dispose in the manner it is, and of this nation and Ireland too, there is nothing further to be said of the Isle of Man, but to refer all to the will of God, and to procure the best conditions you can for yourself and our poor family, and friends there, and those that came over with me ; and so, trusting in the assistance and goodness of God, begin the world again, though near to winter, whose cold and piercing blasts are much more tolerable than the malicious approaches of a poisoned serpent, or an inveterate or malign enemy; from whose power the Lord of Heaven bless and preserve you. God Almighty comfort you and my poor children; and the Son of God, whose blood was shed for our good, preserve your lives, that, by the goodwill and mercy of God, we may meet once more on earth, and at last in the kingdom of heaven, where we shall be for ever free from all rapine, plunder, and violence. And so I rest everlastingly,

" Your most faithful,

" DERBY."*

Lord Derby was fully aware that his life must be sacrificed; he knew how many enemies he had in the town where his trial was to take place. Bradshaw contrived that his son should be one of the judges. Amongst them were also Colonel Birch, who had seized the Earl's daughters at Knowsley, and who never forgot that Lord Derby had once "trailed him under a hay-cart at Manchester," which had procured for him the name of the Earl of Derby's carter; and Colonel Rigby, still smarting under the recollection of his defeat before Latham House. These three were seconded by Sir Richard Houghton, a son of Sir

---

* SEACOME'S *House of Stanley.*

Gilbert Houghton, formerly a friend and follower of the Earl's. This "rebellious son of a very loyal father" united with Bradshaw in representing to Cromwell how very unsafe it would be to suffer so powerful an enemy to live; and a commission was appointed to try him by a pretended court-martial, composed of twelve sequestrators for the county of Chester, under the presidency of Colonel Mackworth, of Shrewsbury. This tribunal was also intended to try Sir Timothy Featherstonehaugh and Captain Benbow, who were both taken, like Lord Derby, with arms in their hands.

On the 1st of October, 1651, the Earl was brought before his judges, accused of a breach of the Act of Parliament passed on the 12th of August, and addressed in the county to Major-General Mitton, prohibiting all correspondence with Charles Stuart or his party, which constituted the crime of high treason, and entailed the punishment of death. When Lord Derby heard the word treason, he exclaimed,—

" I am no traitor; neither——"

" Sir," replied the president, "your words are contemptible. You must be silent during the reading of the Act and your charge." *

The Earl conducted his own defence, for he was allowed neither books nor counsel. He pleaded that,

* *State Trials.*

having received quarter, and not having committed
any other offence since then, he ought not to have
been brought before a court-martial ; and he demanded
to be tried by a civil court; insisting, at the same time,
that, as he was still in the Isle of Man at the date of
publication of the Act cited against him, he had not
and could not have any knowledge of it, and was,
therefore, not responsible for having violated it.

No importance was attached to this last plea ; but a
long and serious discussion took place on the question
of the quarter received, and his appeal to the civil
court.   By his judges he was already condemned ; but
it was necessary to give some colour of justice to the
trial.   They maintained, therefore, that quarter for life
could be granted only to such as were *hostes*, that is,
enemies, not to such as were *perduelles*, or natives ;
that, as such, taken with arms in his hands, fighting
against his country, the Earl of Derby was guilty of
high treason, and merited the punishment of death ;
which sentence was accordingly passed on the 11th of
October, and was ordered to be carried into effect at
Bolton, on the 15th of the same month.

By allowing him so short an interval between his
sentence and his execution, the judges intended to
render impossible any appeal to Parliament ; but Lord
Strange, whose horses had been kept ready saddled

for two days, set off for London as soon as his father's condemnation was known, and, by travelling day and night, reached the end of his journey in twenty-four hours, and sent in his petition to the House through the Speaker, Mr. Lenthal. The appeal was an affecting one. The noble character of the Earl pleaded strongly in his favour ; the Royalist party was so completely crushed as no longer to cause the Government any uneasiness, and the majority of the members present were inclined to mercy. At this critical moment Cromwell and Bradshaw rose and left the House, carrying several of their friends with them ; and, the numbers left not being sufficient to form a House, the petition could not be put to the vote, and the question was thus decided silently, and without appeal.

Lord Strange rode back to Chester, where his father still was, and carried the fatal news to him himself. The Earl embracing him, said :—

" My son, I thank you for your duty, diligence, and best endeavours to save my life ; but since it cannot be obtained, I must submit."

And, kneeling down, he said,—" Domine, non mea voluntas, sed tua."

His chaplain, Mr. Baggerley, who has left us an account of these last hours of the Earl's life, was present when Lord Strange returned.

"Colonel Duckenfeld," said Lord Derby, "wished to persuade me yesterday evening that my life was not in danger. I patiently heard him discourse, but did not believe him, for I was resolved not to be deceived with the vain hopes of this fading world."

He then repeated his instructions to Mr. Baggerley, to whom he had intrusted his letters for the Isle of Man, touching particularly on those articles which he had communicated to the Countess for the surrender of the island, "discoursing with affectionate protestations of his honour and respect for my lady, both for her high birth and goodness as a wife, and much tenderness of his children there, especially my Lady Mary; and was going on, when suddenly came in one Lieutenant Smith, a rude fellow, with his hat on, who told my Lord he came from Colonel Duckenfeld, the Governor, to tell his lordship he must be ready for his journey to Bolton. My Lord replied,—

"'When would you have me to go?'

"'To-morrow, about six in the morning," said Smith.

"'Well,' said my Lord, 'I thank God I am readier to die than for my journey. However, commend me to the Governor, and tell him by that time I will be ready for both.'

" Then that insolent rebel Smith said :—

" ' Doth your lordship know any friend or servant that would do that thing your lordship knows of ? It would do well if you had a friend.'

" ' What do you mean ? ' replied my Lord. ' Would you have me to find one to cut off my own head ? '

" ' My Lord, if you could get a friend——'

" ' Nay, sir,' answered my Lord, ' if those men that will have my head will not find one to cut it off, let it stand where it is. I thank my God my life hath not been so bad that I should be instrumental to deprive myself of it, though He hath been so merciful to me as to be well resolved against the worst of terrors death can put upon me. As for me and my servants, our ways have been to prosecute a just war by honourable and just means, and not those barbarous ways of blood, which to you is a trade.' " *

When Smith withdrew, Lord Derby wrote the following letters to his wife and those of his children who were with her in the Isle of Man :—

" *Chester, October* 12*th*, 1651.

" MY DEAR HEART,—I have heretofore sent you comfortable lines, but, alas ! I have now no word of comfort, saving to our last and best refuge, which is

* *Narrative of Mr. Baggerley, in State Trials.*

Almighty God, to whose will we must submit. And
when we consider how He hath disposed of these
nations and the government thereof, we have no more
to do but to lay our hands upon our mouths, judging
ourselves and acknowledging our sins, joined with
others, to have been the cause of these miseries, and
to call on Him with tears for mercy.

" The Governor of this place, Colonel Duckenfeld,
is General of the Forces which are going now against
the Isle of Man, and however you might do for the
present, in time it would be a grievous and troublesome business to resist, especially those that at this
hour command three nations; wherefore my advice,
notwithstanding my great affection to that place, is,
that you would make conditions for yourself and children, servants, and people there, and such as came
over with me, to the end you may go to some place of
rest where you may not be concerned in war; and
taking thought of your poor children, you may in some
sort provide for them; then prepare yourself to come
to your friends above, in that blessed place where bliss
is, and no mingling of opinions.

" I conjure you, my dearest heart, by all those
graces which God hath given you, that you exercise
your patience in this great and strange trial. If harm
come to you, then I am dead indeed; and until then I

shall live in you, who are truly the best part of myself.
When there is no such as I in being, then look upon
yourself and my poor children ; then take comfort, and
God will bless you.

"I acknowledge the great goodness of God, to
have given me such a wife as you ; so great an honour
to my family, so excellent a companion to me, so pious,
so much of all that can be said of good. I must confess it impossible to say enough thereof. I ask God
pardon, with all my soul, that I have not been enough
thankful for so great a benefit, and when I have done
anything at any time that might justly offend you, with
joined hands I also ask you pardon.

"Baggerley and Paul (Moreau) go by my directions
to tell you my further reasons for the delivery of the
island, according to these desires which you will see
under my hand.

"Oh, my dear soul, I have reason to believe that
this may be the last time that ever I shall write unto
you. I thank you for all your goodness to me ; for
Jesus' sake forgive me when at any time I have not
been good to you. Comfort yourself the best you can.
I must forgive all the world, else I could not go out of
it as a good Christian ought to do ; and I hold myself
in duty bound, and in discretion, to desire you to
forgive my son and his bed-fellow. She hath more

judgment than I looked for, which is not a little pleasing to me, and it may be of good use to him and the
rest of our children. She takes care of him, and I
am deceived much if you and I have not been greatly
misinformed when we were told ill of her. I hope you
will have reason to think so too.

"It will be necessary that the writings concerning
the estates be sent over, to the end my son may put in
his claim betimes. Oh, my dear, again I ask you to
take comfort; when you so do rejoice thereat I beseech
you, as doing me a great favour; and for my sake, keep
not too strict, too severe, a life, but endeavour to live
for your children's sake, which by an over-melancholy
course you cannot do, but both destroy them and yourself, and neglect my last request. The world knows
you so full of virtue and piety that it will never be ill
thought of if you do not keep your chamber, as other
widows who have not reached to that reputation which
you have, and than which there is not a greater upon
earth. I draw near the bottom of the paper, and I am
drawing on to the grave, for presently I must away
to the fatal stroke, which shows little mercy in this
nation, and as for justice the Great Judge judge
thereof.

"I have no more to say to you at this time
than my prayers for the Almighty's blessing to

you, and my dear Mall, Ned, and Billy.   Amen:
sweet Jesu.

" Your faithful

" Derby." *

" My dear Mall, Ned, and Billy,—I remember well
how sad you were to part with me, but now I fear your
sorrow will be greatly increased to be informed that
you can never see me more in this world ; but I charge
you all to strive against too great a sorrow ; you are all
of you of that temper that it would do you much harm.
My desires and prayers to God are that you may have
a happy life.   Let it be as holy a life as you can, and
as little sinful as you can avoid or prevent.

" I can well now give you that counsel, having in
myself, at this time, so great a sense of the vanities of
my life, which fill my soul with sorrow ; yet I rejoice
to remember that when I have blessed God with pious
devotion, it has been most delightful to my soul, and
must be my eternal happiness.

" Love the Archdeacon " (the Rev. Mr. Rutter) ;
" he will give you good precepts.   Obey your mother
with cheerfulness, and grieve her not ; for she is your
example, your nursery, your counsellor, your all under

---

* Printed entire, for the first time, in the publications of the
Cheetham Society, vol. lxvii. p. 227.

God. There never was, nor ever can be, a more deserving person. I am called away, and this is the last I shall write to you. The Lord my God bless and guard you from all evil: so prays your father at this time, whose sorrow is inexorable to part with Mall, Ned, and Billy. Remember

" DERBY."

While Lord Derby wrote these simple farewell words to his wife and children, his son and daughters who had the sad satisfaction of being with him at Chester, were still hoping against hope. As early as the 9th of September, Lady Catherine had written to her aunt, the Duchesse de la Trémoille, as Lord Strange had also done from London, on first hearing the rumour of his father's arrest, even before he had ascertained it as a fact :—

"I hear that he is certainly taken," wrote Lord Strange; "if it is true, there is no hope for him, humanly speaking, but in the Isle of Man, and scarcely even there. The party now in power laugh at that idea, regarding the place as one that is sure to follow the rest of their conquests. Those who have made themselves masters of three kingdoms may well laugh at a refuge like the Isle of Man ; all this makes me despair. If there could be an ambassador sent here to treat of a peace between France and this country, with instructions to speak in favour of my father, perhaps, with God's help, some good might be done. I am sure that your goodness of heart will incline you to do what you can for my father, who has the honour of being so nearly related to you."

The daughter's cry of distress was more tender and pressing :—

" MADAME,— The honour of my relationship to your Highness emboldens me to implore your help in the extremity into which our whole family has been plunged by the arrest of my father, who is now a prisoner in the hands of the Parliament. About five weeks ago he came to this kingdom in the service of his Majesty of Scotland, who also came here in person at the head of an army, which has been completely routed : no one knows what has become of the King ; but my father with many others, of every rank and condition, has been brought to this town, where my sister and I, after two years of imprisonment, have seen him in so miserable a condition that our own is rendered a thousand times more grievous and sorrowful, from our apprehensions of his danger. The thought of this is killing us, and will certainly be the death of my mother when she hears of it, unless she can be assured, at the same time,

of his safety.   She is in the Isle of Man, and I fear she
will not obtain permission to come and help him, which
makes me humbly implore my uncle, and you, Madame,
to have compassion on our sorrow, and to do what you
may judge expedient for my father's preservation and
deliverance : by doing which you will uphold a falling
house, and restore life to my mother and to all her
family, who will never cease to pray to God for the
preservation and prosperity of your Highnesses.   I am,
and will be all my life,

      " Madame, your very humble, obedient,

           and faithful niece and servant,

               " CATHERINE STANLEY."

But Cromwell's judges allowed no time for the
sending of embassies, or for slow diplomatic interven-
tion ; before Madame de la Trémoille could reply to
these letters, Bradshaw had accomplished his revenge.

After writing his last letters to his wife and children, Lord Derby divided what jewels he still possessed,
wrapping them up in several papers, and addressing
them to his friends and servants.

" At night about six," says Mr. Baggerley, " I went
to him again, and as we were talking, the Governor
sent him a second message that he was to be ready
to start at seven o'clock next morning.

" ' I shall not have occasion to go before nine o'clock,' replied his lordship; 'tell the Governor I shall be ready at that hour; if he has earnester occasion he may take his own hour.' "

The Earl wished to take the communion before setting out. His daughters were with him and he desired to enjoy in peace the last moments that he had to devote to his children. He also permitted his daughter-in-law, Lady Strange, to come to him, as her husband wrote a few days afterwards to the Duchesse de la Trémoille :—

" My wife and I have had the consolation of receiving my father's blessing and his pardon for what we have done without his sanction ; and much more than a simple pardon, for before his death he showed as much affection and tenderness for my wife as if she had been his own daughter, and one that he loved dearly, who had never done anything to displease him."

Lord Derby's indignation against his son's marriage had never, indeed, been so great as that of his wife, and in his last hours he was willing to forget all the past. " Forgive us our trespasses as we forgive those that trespass against us."

When his children had left him, he remained alone with Mr. Baggerley, to whom he repeated his instructions and advice.

" I hope," he said, " they that love me will never
forsake my wife and children ; God will be a master
to them and provide for them after my death." Then,
giving the chaplain his letters for the Isle of Man :
" Deliver these," he said, " with my most tender affection, to my wife and sweet children, which shall continue with my prayers for them to the last minute of
my life. I have instructed you as to all things for
your journey; but as to that sad part of it with respect
to them, I can say nothing. Silence, and your own
looks, will best tell your message. The great God
of heaven direct you, and prosper and comfort them,
in this their day of deep affliction and distress."

On the morning before his execution, after taking
the sacrament, Lord Derby spent some time alone at
his devotions, as was his custom. His chaplain has
preserved the following prayer, which he was in the
habit of using every morning :—

" O Almighty Lord God ! thou that hearest prayer,
assist me now in my devotion. By the help of thy
blessed spirit, make me to have so right a sense of my
sins that I may be humbled before thee, and of thy
mercy that I may be raised and comforted by thee.
O Lord, make me tremble to consider thee a most
mighty and terrible God ; and make me again rejoice
to know thee a most loving and merciful Father.

Make me zealous of thy glory, and thankful for thy
bounties; make me know my wants and the frailties
of nature, and be earnest in my prayer that thou will
forgive all my misdeeds; make me in my address to
thee to have a present mind, and no cares, wandering
thoughts, or desires elsewhere, or separate from thee;
make me so to pray, that I may obtain of thee mercy
and the relief of all my necessities; for the sake of thy
blessed Son and my Redeemer, the holy Jesus. Amen."

When he left his closet, Lord Derby took leave
of his companions in misfortune, Sir Timothy Featherstonehaugh, Mr. Crossen, and three other gentlemen,
who were condemned like himself.

"Gentlemen," he said, "God bless and keep you.
I hope now my blood will satisfy for all that were
with me, and that you will in a short time be at
liberty. But if the cruelty of these men will not end
there, be of good comfort; God will strengthen you
to endure to the last, as he hath done me; for you
shall hear that I die like a Christian, a man, a soldier,
and an obedient servant to the most just and virtuous
of princes."

He then rode out of Chester, "the people weeping
all round him." About half a mile from the town,
the Earl, meeting his two daughters, alighted from
his horse, "and with an humble behaviour and noble

carriage, kneeled down beside the coach and prayed·
for them.   Then, rising up, took his leave, and so
parted." " This," says Mr. Baggerley, " was the
deepest scene of sorrow my eyes ever beheld; so
much grief and so much concern and tender affection
on both sides, I never was witness of before."

As they drew near to Leigh, where they were to
spend the night, Lord Derby said to his chaplain,—

" When you come into the Isle of Man, commend
me to the Archdeacon there; tell him I have not
forgotten our conversations on death.   I often said
to him the thoughts of death could not trouble me
in fight with a sword in my hand, but that I feared
it would somewhat startle me tamely to submit to
a blow upon a scaffold.   But tell the Archdeacon
from me, that I do find in myself an absolute change
as to that opinion, and I bless God for it, who hath
put such comfort and courage into my soul, that I can
as willingly lay down my head upon a block as ever
I did upon a pillow."

As he lay down in bed with his face resting upon
his hand, " Methinks," he said, " I lie like a monument
in a church ; and to-morrow I shall really be so."

The last day, Wednesday, 15th of October, had
now arrived, when his journey was to end at the foot
of the scaffold.

" Put on my order once this day," he said to Lord Strange, who held the order of the Garter, which had lately been sent to the Earl by Charles II., before his departure for Holland, "and I will send it to you again by Baggerley; pray return it to my gracious sovereign, when you shall be so happy as to see him, and say I send it with all humility and gratitude, as I received it, spotless and free from any stain, according to the honourable example of my ancestors."

When he was dressed he went to prayers, and had the Decalogue read to him, making his confession at the end of every commandment ; then received abso- lution and the sacrament; after which he called for pen and ink, and wrote his last speech.

Before starting " he drank a cup of beer to the health of all he loved," and would have walked into the church, but he was not permitted, " nor even to ride that day upon his own horse ; but he was set upon a little galloway," the guards fearing that the people would rescue him.

On the way, observing that the wind was easterly, cold, and sharp, Lord Derby turned to his chaplain and said :—

" Baggerley, there is a great difference betwixt you and me now, for my thoughts are fixed, and I know where I shall rest to-night, but you don't; for every

little alteration of wind or weather moves you of this
world.   You must leave me, and go to my wife and
children in the Isle of Man ; but do not leave me, if
possible, until you see me buried as I told you, and
acquaint my dear wife and family with our parting."

About twelve o'clock Lord Derby arrived at
Bolton, accompanied by two troops of horse and one
company of foot, the people everywhere praying and
weeping as he went.

He was taken to a house in the town—for the
scaffold, which was built in great part of timber from
the ruins of Latham House, was not quite ready, the
people of the town having refused to strike a nail or
give any assistance to it, many of them saying :—
"We have suffered many and great losses since the
war began, but none so great as this, that the Earl of
Derby, our lord and patriot, should lose his life here,
and in such a manner."

He spent the time till three o'clock praying and
conversing with his friends ; telling them how he had
lived, how he had prepared for death, and how God
had strengthened him against the terrors of it; then
after giving some good instructions to his son, who
had come with him thus far, he desired to be in
private, where he continued on his knees in prayer for
a good while.   He then called his friends again, and

told them he had no fear of death, "only the care and concern he had what might become of his wife and children after his death was often in his thoughts, and sat heavy upon him ; but now he was satisfied that God would be a husband and a father to them, into whose hands and Almighty protection he committed them."

And so, taking leave of his son, he embraced him, saying :—

" I charge you, upon my blessing, to be ever dutiful to your distressed mother, and ever tender how you in anything grieve or offend her."

Then turning to an officer he told him he was ready.

As he approached the scaffold, which was erected on the site of the old cross, he said :—

" *Venio, Domine.* I come to fulfil thy will, O my God ; this must be my cross ! blessed Saviour, I take it up willingly, and follow thee."

He walked with a firm step through the people, who prayed and wept aloud.

" Good people," said he, " I thank you all, and I beseech you still to pray for me. The God of mercies bless you ; the Son of God establish you in righteousness ; and the Holy Ghost fill you with all comforts."

At the foot of the scaffold he said,—" I am not

afraid to go up here, though to my death : there are
but these few steps between me and eternity."

Then kissing the ladder, he went up; and after
saluting the people, and taking a few turns up and
down, he seated himself at the east end of the scaffold,
and made this address to the people, who pressed
about him :—

" CHRISTIAN GENTLEMEN AND PEOPLE,—

" YOUR business hither to-day is to see a sad
spectacle, a peer of the land to be in a moment un-
manned, and cut off by an untimely end.   And though
truly, if my general course of life were but inquired
into, I may modestly say there is such a moral honesty
upon it, as some may be so peremptory as to expostu-
late why this great judgment has fallen upon me.   But
know that I am able to give them and myself an
answer, and out of this breast" (laying his hand upon
his heart) "to give a better account of my judgment
and execution than my judges themselves or you are
able to give.   It is God's wrath upon me for sins long
unrepented of, many judgments withstood, and mercies
slighted ; therefore God hath whipped me by His
severe rod of correction, that he might not lose me.
I pray join with me in prayer that it may not be a
fruitless rod ; that when by this rod I have laid down

my life, by this staff I may be comforted and received into glory.

" As for my accusers, I am sorry for them—they have committed Judas's crime ; but I wish and pray for them Peter's tears, that by Peter's repentance they may escape Judas's punishment ; and I wish other people so happy they may be taken up betimes, before they have drunk more blood of Christian men, possibly less deserving than myself.

" It is true there have been several addresses made for mercy; and I will put the obstruction of it upon nothing more than upon my own sin, and seeing God sees it not fit (I having not glorified Him in my life), I might do it in my death, which I am content to do. I profess, in the face of God, no particular malice to any one of the State or Parliament ; to do them a bodily injury I had none.

" For the cause in which I had a great while waded, I must needs say my engagement or continuance in it hath laid no scruple upon my conscience. It was on principles of law, the knowledgment whereof I embrace, and on principles of religion, my judgment satisfied and conscience rectified, that I have pursued those ways, for which, I bless God, I find no backwardness upon my conscience; nor have I put it into the bead-roll of my sins.

"I will not presume to decide controversies. I desire God to honour Himself in prospering that side that hath right with it, and that you may enjoy peace and plenty when I shall enjoy peace and plenty beyond all you possess here. In my conversation with the world I do not know where I have an enemy with cause, or that there is such a person to whom I have a regret; but if there be any whom I cannot recollect, under the notion of Christian men, I pardon them as freely as if I had named them by name. I freely forgive them, being in free peace with all the world, as I desire God, for Christ's sake, to be at peace with me. For the business of death, it is a sad sentence in itself if men consult with flesh and blood; but truly, without boasting, I say it; or if I do boast, I boast in the Lord, I have not to this minute had one consultation with the flesh about the blow of the axe, or one thought of the axe more than as to my passport to glory.

"I take it for an honour, and I owe thankfulness to those under whose power I am that they have sent me hither, to a place, however, of punishment, yet of some honour, to die a death exceeding worthy of my blood, answerable to my birth and qualification; and this courtesy of theirs hath much helped towards the pacification of my mind.

"I shall desire God that those gentlemen in that sad bead-roll to be tried by the High Court of Justice, that they may find that really there that is nominal in the Act, an high court of justice, a court of high justice, high in its righteousness, though not in its severity. 'Father forgive them, and forgive me as I forgive them.'

"I desire that you would pray for me, and not give over praying till the hour of death, nor till the minute of death, for the hour is come already; that, as I have a very great load of sins, so I may have the wings of your prayers, to help those angels that are to convey my soul to heaven, hoping this day to see Christ in the presence of the Father, and myself there to rejoice with all other saints and angels for evermore.

"One thing more I desire to be clear in. There lieth a common imputation upon the King's party that they are Papists, and under that name we are made odious to those of the contrary opinion. I am not a Papist; but renounce the Pope, with all his dependencies. When the distractions in religion first sprang up, I might have been thought apt to turn from this Church to the Roman; but was utterly unsatisfied in their doctrine, in point of faith, and very much as to their discipline. The religion which I profess is that

which passeth under the name of Protestant, though
that be rather a name of distinction than properly
essential to religion. But the religion which was
found out in the Reformation purged from all the
errors of Rome, in the reign of Edward VI., practised
in the reigns of Queen Elizabeth, King James, and
King Charles, that blessed prince deceased; that
religion before it was defaced, I am of, which I take
to be Christ's Catholic, though not the Roman Catholic
religion; in the profession and practice whereof I will
live and die.

" Good friends, I die for the King, the laws of the
land, and the Protestant religion——"

At these words, a soldier called out,—

" We have no king, and will have no lords."

This raised a sudden tumult amongst the soldiers,
who rode up and down the streets, cutting and slash-
ing the people as they pressed round the scaffold.

" What is the matter, gentlemen ? " said the Earl.
" Whom do you seek ? I fly not, and here is none to
pursue you."

The soldiers desisted ; but quietness could not be
restored. Lord Derby tried to continue his address ;
but finding it impossible, he turned to one of his
servants, and gave him the manuscript, saying,—

" I will speak to my God, who I know will hear

me ; and when I am dead, let the world know what I
would have said."

Then he called to the headsman, and asked if he
was ready.

" Not quite, my Lord," replied the man, with a
surly air.

" I am not angry with thee, friend," said the Earl ;
" thou art not the hand that throws the stone."

The bystanders called to the executioner to ask
his lordship's pardon, but he seemed unwilling ; upon
which Lord Derby said,—

" Friend, I give thee the pardon thou wilt not
ask." Then, handling the rough furred coat the man
had on, he said,—" This will be troublesome to thee.
I pray thee put it off as willingly as I put off this gar-
ment of my flesh, that is now so heavy for my soul."

The executioner made his preparations so slowly
that the Earl murmured,—

" How long, O Lord, how long ! You see I am
ready, but the block is not," said he to one of his chaplains, whom he saw moving about amongst the crowd.
" When I am got into my chamber " (pointing to his
coffin), " I shall then be at rest, and no longer troubled
with such a guard and noise as I have been."

Then, turning to the crowd, he said :—

" Good people, I thank you for your prayers and

your tears; I have heard the one and seen the other; the God of heaven hear your supplications for me, and mine for you, through the mediation of Christ our Saviour."

He caused the block to be turned towards the church, saying,—

" I will look towards thy sanctuary whilst I am here ; and I know that in a few minutes I shall behold my God and my King in thy sanctuary above. Under the shadow of thy wings shall be my rest till this calamity be overpast."

On seeing the block,—

" That methinks is very low," he said, "and yet there is but one step betwixt that and heaven."

Then taking the axe into his hands he kissed it, and said,—

" Thou canst not hurt me, for I fear thee not."

He then removed his doublet, and asked how he should place himself.

" I have been called a bloody man," said he, " yet, truly, I never yet had that severe curiosity to see any put to death in peace."

The executioner told him to put up his hair, and he knelt down and prayed privately a good while; after repeating the Lord's prayer, aloud, he rose and said smilingly,

" My soul is now at rest, and so shall my body be
.immediately. The Lord bless my King, and restore
him to his right in this kingdom, and the Lord bless
this kingdom and restore them to their rights in their
King, that he and they may join hand to hand to settle
truth and peace. And the Lord bless this country,
this town, and this people. The Lord comfort my sad
wife and children, and reward all my friends with peace
and happiness, both here and hereafter. And the Lord
forgive them who were the cause and authors of this
my sad end and unjust death ; for so it is as to man-
kind, though before God I deserve much more. But I
hope that my sins are all washed in the blood of Jesus
Christ."

Then laying his head upon the block, he said to the
executioner,—

" Wait till I give you a sign. The Lord bless my
wife and children ; the Lord bless us all. Blessed be
God's gracious name for ever and ever. Amen. Let
the whole earth be filled with his glory. Amen."

He lifted his hand, but the executioner either did
not observe it or was not ready ; and the Earl rose
again, saying,—

" Why do you keep me from my Saviour ? What
have I done that I die not, and that I may live with
him ? "

And, placing his head again upon the block, he repeated the same words; then, lifting up his hands, the axe fell, and separated his head from his body.*

There were no sounds of triumph; the soldiers dispersed silently, and nothing was heard but the sobs of women and children, for the grief of the men was dumb, like their anger.

* SEACOME'S *House of Stanley. Narrative of Mr. Baggerley. State Trials.*

CHAPTER VIII.

WIDOWHOOD.

WHILE Mr. Baggerley, faithfully carrying out Lord Derby's instructions, was accompanying his son to Ormskirk, to see his body placed in the tomb of his ancestors, Lady Derby was still in the Isle of Man, ignorant of the blow about to fall upon her. Communication with the island was carried on with difficulty, and news travelled slowly. Before she had received her husband's first letter telling her of his capture, he was already dead.

She had been making preparations for the defence of the island which was so dear to them both, and had fortified the castle of Russen, a place situated upon a high and almost impregnable rock, where was kept the leaden crown, the distinctive mark of the independent royalty of the Isle of Man, when, one day, Captain Young arrived on board the frigate *President*, one of

those ships of the enemy which, as she had written to
the Duchesse de la Trémoille, harassed their coasts,
and summoned her to surrender the Isle of Man in the
name of the Parliament.

" I hold it by commission from my Lord," she
replied, " and I will not give it up without orders
from him, being obliged by my duty to obey the
instructions of my husband."

Before any such instructions reached her she heard
of his death.   We do not know who undertook to
carry her the mournful intelligence ; whether she learnt
it from Mr. Baggerley, or whether her son ventured
to bring the news to her himself.   From a sentence
in one of her letters, dated the 22nd of March, 1652,
we are rather led to infer that she learnt her misfortune only on the arrival of her enemies, and from
their lips.   However this may be, she continued to
hold the Isle of Man, and when Colonels Duckenfeld
and Birch, with a commission from the Parliament,
arrived on the coasts and demanded the surrender
of her little kingdom, she replied that she held it for
the King, and would not give it up to his enemies,
without his orders.

It was now about the end of October ; Charles II.
had taken refuge in France, and the Royalist cause
seemed lost without hope of recovery.   All towns

and castles holding for the King had surrendered to the Parliament; but the intrepid daughter of the Trémoilles and the Nassaus still held her islands in the King's name, and refused to give them up without his authority.

She placed herself and her children under the protection of Sir Thomas Armstrong, who had been appointed governor of Russen Castle by Lord Derby. His brother commanded Peele Castle, and the forces of the Isle of Man were intrusted to Captain William Christian, a native of the country, and a son of Captain Edward Christian, who had formerly held a high place in Lord Derby's esteem. He had, in fact, for some time been governor of the island; but Lord Derby had reason to be dissatisfied with his services, and had appointed Captain Greenhalgh in his place. He, however, continued his favours to the family of Christian, and after the father's death he intrusted to the son, William Christian, the charge of such troops as he left behind him in the island when he went to join Charles II. in England. But the son proved as ungrateful and faithless as the father. The malice of Lord Derby's enemies was not satisfied even by his death; Bradshaw desired the destruction of his family, and Rigby hoped to be revenged on the heroine who had humbled him before Latham. They succeeded in gaining over Christian, who permitted the Parliamentarian troops to land on the island during the night. The soldiers had been bribed and offered no resistance; and on the following day the garrisons of both the castles revolted against their governors, who were taken prisoners by Christian, and, with the Countess and her children, were delivered into the hands of the Parliamentarian commissioners.

"These, Madame, are the conditions under which Captain Christian has delivered up the island," said Birch, ironically, offering Lady Derby a paper, in which no mention was made of her rights nor of her son's rights over this hereditary kingdom of the Derbys. Glancing at it, she said, with her accustomed courage,—

"No place is mentioned here but the Isle of Man; the neighbouring islands have not surrendered; permit me to retire to Peele Castle" (on one of the adjacent islands) "with my children, that I may rest there until I can pass over into France or Holland, and find a place to lay my head."

This, which she asked as a favour when she might have claimed it as a right, was not granted; the Isle of Man, of the hereditary possession of which she and her children were to be deprived, was to be their prison for two months longer; and it was only in the following December, as we learn from a letter of her son to the Duchesse de la Trémoille, that she at length obtained permission to go to England, where she hoped to find shelter and sympathy.

" She who had brought fifty thousand pounds sterling of dowry to this nation," says the historian of the House of Stanley, " had not even a morsel of bread to eat, and owed everything to the favour of friends almost as distressed as herself."

The first letter which we have from Lady Derby after her long silence is dated from London on the 25th of March, 1652 :—

" Dear Sister,—In all my heavy trials I have desired nothing so much as the honour of your letters, which were so full of friendship for this unhappy one, and of compassion for the misfortunes I have suffered, that, I confess, if my grief were not inconsolable, you would have relieved it. But alas! dear sister, there is nothing left for me but to mourn and weep, since all my joy is in the grave. I look with astonishment at myself that I am still alive after so many misfortunes; but God has been pleased to sustain me wonderfully, and I know that without his help I could never have survived all my miseries. To tell you all would be too distressing ; but, in short, dear

sister, I have endured all the sharpest sorrows that
could be conceived, and they were announced to
me by the destroyers of my happiness, with all imaginable particulars to overwhelm me. It is in this
that I have experienced the wonderful assistance of
my God, that I did not despair as, humanly speaking,
stronger minds than my own might have done; but
His providence supported me, and led me in my
misery to adore His goodness towards me; and to
magnify Him in my sorrow for the noble end of that
glorious martyr who showed such wonderful constancy
—nothing shaking him in the least but the thought
of the wretched condition in which he foresaw I should
be. In his last letters he gave me far greater proofs
of his affection than I had any right to expect, and
his last request was that I would live and take care of
his children. This thought alone sustains me in my
afflictions; for my son the Earl of Derby does nothing
to comfort me, both he and his wife showing great
bitterness of feeling towards me. But this is the will
of God to wean me altogether from the world, and to
show me its vanities. If I were not obliged for my
children's sake to look after my affairs, which are in
such an uncertain state, I should no longer have any
concern with the world. It is true that in one of their
courts, after incredible trouble, I have succeeded in

getting my marriage contract allowed, which settled on me, besides my dowry, certain estates bought with my own money, which is all that I have for my five children. I must, however, obtain the authorisation of another of their courts, in order to receive the revenue of the estates, and it is here that my enemies endeavour to prove me guilty; if this should happen, it will be necessary to present a petition to Parliament, which is a very difficult and tedious thing. But I have reason to think that I shall obtain what I desire; the most influential people tell me to hope. God has hitherto blessed my endeavours, and has given me both friends and means of subsistence; for I have lost all my personal property, having had only 400 crowns worth of silver plate allowed me to bring me here from the Isle of Man, and nothing more since that. You see, then, the unhappy condition to which my life is reduced; I wish to end it with you, but I cannot yet tell what will become of me. . . . . If I could get the produce of what has already been granted to me, I should have the means of bringing up my children in a manner befitting their birth, my two youngest sons* being of great promise, healthy, tall and well-grown for their age, and studious, especially the younger, who, I think, will be a good scholar. If it please God

* They both died young and unmarried.

to bless them and make them worthy of their father,
they will doubtless feel how much honoured they are
by their connection with so many illustrious persons."

A good and virtuous reputation counts for something even in human affairs. Lady Derby's next letter
proves that her embarrassed circumstances did not
prevent her from marrying her children "according to
their birth."

" I have something very different to tell you of,
that is, a suitor for your niece Catherine : thus you
see that God does not forsake His children. I was
very far from thinking of such a marriage in our
poverty, or indeed of any marriage. The gentleman is the Marquis of Dorchester. He has been
married before, but has only two daughters. He is
a Protestant, aged forty-four ; sensible, clever, accomplished, and rich, having fourteen thousand a year, his
brothers and sisters provided for, and ready money in
his purse. The best and highest alliances in England
have been offered to him, and yet he has sought us
out. I shall not be able to give her anything until my
affairs are settled ; but this alliance will help us not a
little. The business was concluded in three days, and I
was obliged to promise to keep it secret till everything
was arranged, otherwise I should have been unwilling
to conclude it without your consent, and that of Mon-

sieur my brother. I crave your pardon for this, but you know, dear sister, what risks letters run in these times; and if the matter had been discovered before all was concluded, many difficulties would have been put in the way. Certain people have attempted this, especially his next brother, who has sons, and who believed that he would never marry. God has sent this good fortune to us; and I implore His blessing on them both : they will be married, I think, in a month. He has given her a ring and a bracelet-clasp, worth ten thousand crowns. She will be a rich woman. Her father was so intimate with him that they called each other brother; but I never saw him before. I hope that God will provide as well for the others who are in my charge. I know of nothing in them but what is good and agreeable. As for my eldest, I cannot say as much for him; he is worse than the prodigal son : and I often think of what that martyr said to me about him before he went to France,—that he had no good opinion of him; 'for,' said that sainted soul, 'he has no shame for his faults, and I never saw him blush for anything that he did.' Alas! I deluded myself; but his father knew him better than I did. There never was so malignant a nature as that woman's, who has nothing good or pleasant about her."

We willingly excuse Lady Derby's joy at seeing her daughter "a rich woman," for she herself had suffered all her life from embarrassed circumstances, although occupying so high a position, and she was now reduced to actual poverty. But if her friend, M. du Plessis-Mornay, had been still alive, he would have reminded her that "(wealth was the last thing that should be thought of in a marriage. L What is most important is the moral character of the person with whom one's life is to be spent; and, above all, that he should fear God.")

The Marquis of Dorchester was possibly without this fear of God, for his wife was not happy. Only three months after the marriage, her mother wrote :—

" I have not made her so happy as I expected; I was led to hope for better things : but what consoles me is that she behaves with admirable wisdom and patience ; and, certes, she is gaining an unexampled reputation."

Lady Dorchester had only one daughter, who died in infancy.

While Lady Derby was thus occupied with her daughter's marriage, war had broken out between France and Holland. The struggle was obstinate, and skilfully conducted by the ablest men of their time,—Blake, Van Tromp, Ruyter, Corneille de Witt;

but it was carried on with very unequal resources in the two countries; and, after two years of mingled reverses and successes, Holland confessed herself beaten.

" Why should I hold my tongue any longer ?" said Corneille de Witt, in July, 1653, in a full assembly of the States,—" I am here in the presence of my rulers. It is my duty to tell them that the English are now masters of us and of the seas."

A few months later the States-General obtained from Cromwell an honourable peace. On one point alone he was not to be moved: he would have no ally of the house of Stuart in power in Holland ; and he demanded that the young Prince William, and the whole house of Nassau, should be excluded for ever from the Stadtholdership. The States resisted this insolent attempt to regulate the internal affairs of their country. Cromwell persisted in demanding from Jean de Witt at least the special consent of the province of Holland, believing that this province was strong enough to force its opinions upon the other members of the confederation. After much hesitation, the States of the province of Holland acceded to Cromwell's demands, and the treaty was concluded on the 5th of June, 1654.

Cromwell had now possessed himself of absolute

power in England. On the 30th of April, after a
violent scene in the House of Commons, he drove out
the members, bidding them begone, for they were no
longer a Parliament; and, locking the doors behind
him, he said to the officers who surrounded him :—
" I did not think to do what I have done to-day; but
I felt the Spirit of God so strong upon me, that I could
no longer give ear to flesh and blood."

He had long been striving to free himself from all
restraints to his power, and he now elected no new
members, but called together, by his own warrant, a
council composed of 139 persons, whom, at the end of
a few months, he dismissed as they had been con-
voked. Four days after the dissolution of December,
1654, he received from the army the title of Lord •
Protector of England, Scotland, and Ireland, a title
which he accepted without eagerness, and by which he
became virtually Sovereign of Great Britain.

Lady Derby had just sent her second son to her
sister-in-law in France.

On the 14th of May, 1654, she wrote :—

" I send you, in this dear child, one of the best
parts of myself; I pray that God will bless him, and
make him acceptable to you. He is very anxious to
please you, and I have commanded him to obey,
reverence, and love you as he does myself. He is

gentle, and of a good disposition, brave, but without pride, a very common vice of his nation. His valet-de-chambre is a gentleman whose father is so much attached to our poor family that he desires his son should be with him, rather than in another position where he might have greater external advantages. He has some knowledge of mathematics, painting, and surveying. His footman is a very useful person, and will do well whatever is given him to do."

In later times, during the French Revolution, it was not usual for the members of the great fallen families to be so well attended. Lady Derby's reasonable complaints must not prevent us from rendering justice to her enemies. The correspondence which is here published absolutely refutes those traditions, which have become almost historical, concerning the treatment to which Lord Derby's family were subjected after his execution. It has been said and printed everywhere that the Countess was kept a prisoner in an unhealthy dwelling in the Isle of Man; that she there lost two of her children; and that she was not released from captivity till the restoration of Charles II. So far from this being the case, we see, from the indisputable evidence of her own letters, that although poor, and deprived of all the luxuries natural to her rank, she was at least free, living in London,

demanding justice, and in a measure obtaining it, sending her son to Paris with suitable attendants, and
marrying her daughters in a rank worthy of their
birth.

On the 12th of March, 1655, Lady Derby
wrote :—

" I think your nephew will have told you of his
sister's * marriage, about which she and her brother
wrote to him last week. With God's blessing I have
every reason to hope for the greatest comfort from it,
he being a very worthy man, who has an unbounded
affection as well as the highest esteem for his wife; she
is, I think, very happy. I am sure that if my daughter
Strafford had the honour of being known to you, she
would also have that of pleasing you. She is quite a
French woman, speaks French better than I do, and
writes it as she does English. I pray that God may
bless them all."

The narrowness of her means very soon obliged
Lady Derby to leave London and return to Knowsley.

" You may believe, dear sister," she writes on the
1st of June, 1655, " how changed I find everything in
this place, never having been here since my troubles;
and how cruelly it recalls to my mind my past happiness, and makes my present sorrows press more heavily

---

* Lady Mary Stanley married the Earl of Strafford.

than ever upon me. God, however, will not forsake me ; but will strengthen me of His goodness. In the midst of my sadness He has been pleased to send me the good news of the birth of your grandson, for which I thank Him, and pray that you may derive from it all the happiness that I wish you. As for my affairs they are in so bad a state, my debts being so great, that I am obliged to live here, and to reduce my expenses to suit my poor condition, in order to pay them if possible."

And some months afterwards :—

" I know not if you have heard of the Protector's last proclamation, in which new taxes are imposed on all those whose estates have been in the hands of the Parliament, and who have paid large sums to recover them. I had hoped that in the poor condition to which it has pleased God to reduce me, and by not interfering in anything whatever but what regards my own little property, I should not to be reckoned in that number ; but I am assured that I am one of them, and everything I have in the world is mortgaged to pay my debts. The sum now demanded is the tenth part of the value of the estates, and the fifteenth part of the personal property ; but I hope I shall not have to pay for more than I possess, which is next to nothing. The good God will not forsake me; as He has had

compassion on me in all my troubles, so He will
continue to befriend me."

This measure of Cromwell's was a general one;
" it was an act of political excommunication against the
Royalists," says M. Guizot, " whether as actual conspirators, or because of their avowed hostility and
secret connivance with conspirators."

" They accuse my mother of speaking against the
Government of this country," Lady Mary Stanley had
written to her aunt in the preceding year; "and
always shut the mouths of those who feel pity for her
condition and ask for some kind of justice for her,
by telling them that she has defied their authority,
without being able to prove anything of the kind, and
without listening to those who could and would vindi-
cate her."

At the same time, all who had served the late
King or his sons were obliged to leave London,
and many Royalists of condition were thrown into
prison.

" Every day new people are suspected," wrote Lady
Derby, " and the prisons receive fresh inmates. In
my present condition I dare not venture to make any
inquiries.   God grant that all may turn to His glory,
and give me grace to submit to whatever He pleases
to send me.   The loss of my property has never been

so hard to bear; but it is my irreparable losses that
overwhelm me."

Lady Derby's greatest anxiety at this time was for
her youngest sons. In her letters to her sister-in-law
she speaks of her concern about the one who was in
France, who seems to have been treated harshly and
without consideration by his valet-de-chambre, who
was also, to some extent, his tutor.

"I am in constant anxiety about him and his
brother," she wrote on the 16th of November, 1655;
"the latter is clever and intelligent; he learns well,
and conducts himself with discretion. May the Lord
preserve them and look on them with compassion; and
may you, dear sister, look kindly on him who has the
honour of being with you. He is of a gentle and somewhat melancholy disposition; and if he is frightened, as
Daguedel tells me he is, and does not dare to speak, I
fear he will become incapable of doing anything. I
am afraid there is some want of discretion on Daguedel's
part; and all who see his letters think as I do."

At length she sent her faithful Trioche to France,
who dismissed Daguedel, and found for his young
master a less arrogant valet-de-chambre.

"Trioche will tell you that my affairs are in a very
bad state, so that I am unwilling to trouble you with
them. I have been taxed on 8,000 livres more of rent

than I receive. The Major-General, the person
who manages everything in the provinces where he
is in command, would not listen to my agent, or
to any one who, like him, had received the rents
from the time that they were in the hands of the
Parliament. He asserted that I had great estates
beyond the sea (as he expressed it), and many jewels
and other imaginary things, and would hear nothing
in my behalf, nor treat with any one who came from
me. We have reason to hope that commissioners will
be appointed in London, with power to redress these
abuses, and also to exempt from payment those whom
they had supposed it necessary to tax. I have presented a petition to the Protector, but it has not yet
been answered. Many people of large property, who
are good Catholics, have been exempted. Everything,
however, would be endurable if they had left us the
free exercise of our religion ; but that is most strictly
forbidden. It is the same religion as that professed
in the time of Henry VIII., and of his daughter
Mary, who made all suffer martyrdom who adhered
to it ; and my mother believed it to be that of the
primitive Church. She never failed to attend prayers,
and had the English liturgy translated into French,
and commanded me to conform to it, and to the admi-
nistration of the sacraments ; as I have done, and will

continue to do, with God's blessing, to the end of my days. And it was one of the last wishes of my husband that his children should be brought up in this creed."

Cromwell had, in fact, been forced by the passions of his party, against his own will and personal feeling, to forbid absolutely the exercise of the Anglican worship. For his own part, indeed, he was inclined to protect the Anglican Church : " its political maxims and strict discipline suited him." He, therefore, allowed his order against chaplains and preceptors to be almost entirely neglected ; "though he could neither refuse it to the fanaticism of his party, nor publicly revoke it in the name of that liberty of conscience which it was his glory to sustain." *

Another family trouble now distressed Lady Derby. Her nephew, the Prince de Tarente, was a warm adherent of the Prince de Condé, and had been formerly attached to his suite in the Fronde. When his brave leader was thrown into prison he left France, and entered the service of the Low Countries ; but returning home in 1655, he was himself arrested, whilst the Prince de Condé was fighting against his country in the Spanish army.

" I have heard with great sorrow of the imprisonment of your son," wrote the Countess. " I have since

* M. GUIZOT, *La Republique et Cromwell.*

learnt from Trioche that his life is not in danger, for
which I bless God. . . . I do not doubt that, with
God's help, for which I pray, he will soon recover
his liberty."

M. de Tarente was detained for several years in
prison, only recovering his liberty in 1660.

Cromwell had now reached the summit of his greatness; one step alone remained to be taken, and for this
he prepared with his accustomed prudence and vigour.
Several Parliaments had met and been dismissed
without the fitting occasion presenting itself in which
to attempt the final blow. At length, in 1657, he
believed that the opportunity for which he waited
had arrived. A petition was presented to him by the
House, modestly entitled, "A humble petition and
advice," entreating him to accept the title of King,
and to take upon him the entire government of the
country. Conferences were held between Cromwell
and the Parliamentary Commissioners, all the proceedings of which were public. It was not the Parliament
alone, but the country, that had to be convinced,—that
party who had effected the Revolution and raised him
to his present power. Even in his own family, the
measure was vehemently opposed by his brother-
in-law, Desborough, and his son-in-law, Fleetwood,
who would not admit the advisability of the step. The

excitement in the army was increasing and becoming serious. It was said that Cromwell was resolved to take no notice of it, and to proceed, when Parliament was called at Whitehall to receive the final answer of the Protector. He accepted all the power which the petition offered him, but refused the title of King, that "feather in his cap" which he had so longed for, and without which he knew neither his work nor his family could take root in England. Once more his hopes were disappointed; his natural caution had arrested him on the edge of the precipice, but his indomitable perseverance never renounced the hope of attaining the object of his desires.

"You have seen by the papers what they have added to the power of the Protector," writes Lady Derby, on the 17th of July, 1657. "It is said his own party are not satisfied. For my part I know nothing about it."

The new political organization proposed in the petition, and adopted on the 7th of May by Cromwell, demanded the construction of an " Other House," as it was styled by those who still hated the title of Lords.

The Protector at once busied himself in forming it, summoning some of the old peers, a certain number of members of the House of Commons, a few of the

highest of the general officers, a few country gentlemen and rich citizens ; in all sixty-three persons. But
these did not all respond to the call. The Commons, so
lately all-powerful, reluctantly accepted this division of
the authority that was henceforth to be shared by the
three orders of the State, while Cromwell's declining
health gave occasion for a formidable opposition to
arise.

" There are so many different opinions about the
Parliament that I know not what to think of it," writes
Lady Derby, in February, 1658. " The House of
Commons vigorously opposes the other House. It is
said the army is approaching London. God will guide
all for His glory and for the good of those who desire
it." She did not know that before she wrote this
Cromwell had dissolved the Parliament. (4th of
February, 1658.)

The argument he employed in explaining his
conduct was, that dissensions in the Government were
dangerous to the safety of the Republic, now, more
than ever, threatened by the friends of Charles Stuart.
This danger was doubtless intentionally exaggerated
to further his own interested schemes ; he said, " there
are nothing but Royalist plots in all parts of the
kingdom."

" We know little news," wrote Lady Derby, in

April 1658, " as it is dangerous to ask for any. We live in times in which the most insignificant person may do harm, and very few have the power to do good. The Scotch rumours have come to London, but I think they are without much foundation. They say another Parliament ought to be called there. Meanwhile numbers of people are thrown into prison, and amongst them, it seems to me, are many who need not, and do not, think of anything but living peaceably at home ; but every one is suspected."

A large number of arrests and eight executions had just given evidence of the vigilance and the alarm of Cromwell. The tears of his favourite daughter, Lady Claypole, could not extract from him the pardon of Sir Henry Slingsby, or of Dr. Hewitt, a distinguished Anglican minister, whose preaching she had frequently attended in secret. This favourite daughter died on the 6th of August, and grief for her loss, operating on Cromwell's already shattered health, threw him on a bed of sickness. All England was startled by the news.

Even to his enemies Cromwell was the representative of organized power and public order. If he should die, the country, they believed, would fall back into a state of anarchy. It was not even known if he had appointed his successor. Many prayers for him

rose up; his own were very fervent. His religious faith
had seldom arrested him in his resolute course towards
any precise object; he had often employed pious
expressions or religious motives as a potent means
of working upon men; nevertheless he believed, and
at the last moment, as Archbishop Tillotson says,
"religious enthusiasm took the place of hypocrisy."
He was dying, in spite of the confidence of those who
had prayed to God to cure him. He felt it himself,
but the desire to live surmounted every other feeling
in his breast. "Lord," he prayed aloud, "though I
am a miserable and wretched creature, I am in
covenant with Thee through grace. And I may and
will come to Thee for Thy people. Thou hast made
me, though very unworthy, a mean instrument to do
them some good, and Thee service; and many of
them have set too high a value on me, though others
wish and would be glad of my death; Lord, however
Thou do dispose of me, continue to go on to do good
for them. . . . . Teach those who look too much on
Thy instruments to depend more upon Thyself. Pardon
such as desire to trample upon the dust of a poor
worm, for they are thy people too. And pardon the
folly of this short prayer, even for Christ's sake. And
give us a good night if it be Thy pleasure. Amen."

Part of this prayer was granted. The day dawned.

It was the 3rd of September, the anniversary of his victories at Dunbar and Worcester. When they offered him something to drink—" It is not my design to drink or sleep," said he ; " but my design is to make what haste I can to be gone." By four o'clock he was dead.

CHAPTER IX.

THE YEAR BEFORE THE RESTORATION.

LADY Derby was but little disturbed by this great event, which threw all England into confusion; she did not see in it the omen of the restoration of the King; she did not perhaps understand that the feeble hands of Richard Cromwell were unfit to wield the heavy sceptre bequeathed to him by his father. She lived retired and alone, and was, besides, at this time much occupied about a negotiation for the marriage of her daughter Amelia with the Earl of Athol.

Cromwell died on the 3rd of September, 1658, and it was only on the 5th April, 1659, that the Countess of Derby wrote, " The news about the Parliament is changed. It speaks with little respect of the late Protector, and has liberated all those whom he put in prison. I know not yet what will come of it." And then she turns at once to the subject nearest her heart : " Two days ago this Scotch nobleman arrived here. He is the Earl of Athol. I think him good-looking and agreeable. I do not yet know your niece's opinion of him. She is so obedient and gentle that I know she will do what I wish ; but I would desire nothing that she disliked. God will direct me for her good. This gentleman has a rent-roll of 30,000*l.* M. d'Athol was made an earl by James I. of Scotland, and the house has been allied with the royal family. His surname is Maure,* and he is the head of this family; in which there are several noble-men."

The Countess returns several times with tender pleasure to the charms of her daughter. " She is an agreeable-looking brunette," she says, " with an equal and patient temper. She has plenty of intellect, and will never vex those to whom she owes respect."

The marriage was at length accomplished. The Countess of Athol lived happily, and had several children ; but she resided in Scotland, and hence-forward her mother saw less of her than of her other children.

---

* The family name of the Earls afterwards Dukes of Athol is Murray. Lady Derby is confused in her mind about proper names.

The affairs of the family were at last partially settled. In 1657 the Parliament had ratified an Act passed by the Barebones Parliament, which secured to the Earl of Derby a revenue of 500*l.* sterling, for himself and his heirs. Another Act decreed him forests in Ireland of the value of nine or ten thousand pounds. " This noble family is among the most unfortunate in England," Major Brooke had said during the discussion. " Justice and charity invite you to confirm this Act," said Lord Broghill. " The poor gentleman has suffered sufficiently, and for the faults of his father ; for I never heard that he himself had committed any crime." " The family is in great distress," said the Master of the Rolls. " It would be right to pass the Bill, if it were only for the consolation of the lady, a foreigner, who belongs to an honourable family." The recommendation of the Master of the Rolls doubtless referred to Charlotte de la Trémoille, and not to Helen de Rupa. The Bill was passed ; but the Countess Dowager does not speak of it. She remained a stranger to the affairs of her son, who was living at Latham, which he had in part rebuilt. She still loved him, however, as we shall very soon see.

In the month of May, 1659, the army demanded from Richard Cromwell the dissolution of the only freely-elected Parliament that England had possessed since the death of Charles I. The power gained by the father escaped from the feeble hands of the son, and the remainder of the Long Parliament, driven out by Cromwell without having ever accepted its dissolution, came back to sit at Westminster, passionately resolved to re-establish that Republic for which it had risked and suffered so much. It counted on the support of the army, which had recalled it, and which was soon to prove its master.

The weakness and disunion of their enemies re-awakened the hopes of the Royalists, so long crushed under the powerful hand of Cromwell. A formidable conspiracy had spread its meshes all over England, and the King and the Duke of York held themselves in readiness to cross the Channel as soon as the plot was ripe; but the treachery of one of its agents rendered it abortive. The Royalist leaders, alarmed by the precautions that had just been taken by the Government, remained quiet. One Presbyterian gen-tleman of the county of Chester, Sir George Booth, alone took up arms as he had promised. The Earl of Derby, Charlotte de la Trémoille's son, engaged with him in this movement, and was, like him, defeated by Lambert, whom, notwithstanding their recent dis-agreements, the Parliament had placed at the head of their troops. The two Royalist leaders were taken as they were trying to escape, and thrown into prison.

" It is only a few days since I performed the duty of writing to you," said Lady Derby to her sister-in-law on the 16th of September, 1659. " I thought you were at Thouars, as you had been pleased to tell me. I told you about the troubles we have had, and how they were relieved by the diligence of Mr. Lambert, who has used his victory most gently. I addressed my entreaties to you for my son Derby, who had been engaged in that unfortunate affair unknown to me, for I have for long been a stranger to everything that concerns him. You know, dear sister, how he has failed in his duty to me, but the tenderness of a mother is easily aroused when her children are in danger. What fills me with anxiety for my son now is that he is a prisoner in the Castle of Shrewsbury, and in some danger, I am told by his sister Dorchester, who helps him in the management of his affairs. Only two days before he was taken his wife was confined with her ninth child, four of whom are living. She is with him at present, which prevents her from doing anything in his affairs. They write me from London that if a letter of recommendation could be sent to M. de Bordeaux it would do much for the preservation of his life, which makes me humbly beg you to have it done for us.   Many people give us great hopes that there is no danger, but others fear the contrary, and in this uncertainty I am not myself."

And some days after : " The governor of Shrews-bury has received orders to take my son to London, where he is just arrived with his wife.   He has had permission to dine with his sister Dorchester, two miles from London, with his guards.   He has not been placed in the Tower of London, but in another prison.   What they will do with him after he is examined I do not know.   It will be a good sign if they return him to the same prison.   He is in no way surprised, and his sister tells me he is in the same mind that he was in before his misfortune.   There are no judges appointed yet for any of them, which makes us hopeful for him and the others ; there are a great many prisoners, amongst whom is the son-in-law of the old Protector" (Lord Falconbridge) " whose wife is with him in the Tower. My son's wife has not done the same, as it was thought she would be more useful in acting outside with my daughter Dorchester and our other friends, than in being with her husband.

" I have not been advised to go to London, or I would have done my utmost for the journey.   My friends have prevented me, for, dear sister, besides

my age and the infirmities attending it, I have no
equipage ; the few horses that my youngest son had
have been taken.   I have had no carriage since my
return from London, where I have never had the
means of keeping more than two horses.   Two of
his children are here with me, and I shall have the
others in a few days, for the little he had for their
support will be taken from them ; and, as things are
at present, he cannot do without help from me.   I
have just had news from my daughter, who tells me
her brother has not been examined yet.   The delay
has been caused by the Parliament and part of the
army being of different opinions ; and the City of
London has presented a petition to the Parliament
for the right of exercising their privilege of choosing
a Mayor.   The Parliament had directed that the last
year's one should be continued, which the said city
believes to be contrary to the custom of all former
times, when absolute power to choose their Mayor
was given them.   It is reported that Mr. Lambert
is displeased at not having received the thanks his
services merit."

On the 13th of October, 1659, Lambert drove the
Long Parliament from Westminster, as Cromwell had
done six years before.   But this time it was not a
step in advance ; the power of the Revolutionists did

not increase, and the internal disorganization of the
Republican party made rapid progress.

" Affairs in this country are not yet as they ought
to be," wrote Lady Derby; but the darkness was soon
to be made light.

Before its fall the Parliament had passed an Act
which threw the Royalists into great anxiety with
regard to that remainder of their possessions which
many successive confiscations had left them.

" I have learnt by this post," wrote Lady Derby
on the 4th of October, 1659, " a thing which, if it is
true, will quite ruin me and more than six thousand
persons. It is an Act which the Parliament has
passed rendering null all the compositions made by
Cromwell's Parliaments. And it is ordered that all
my revenue is to be seized, and that we shall be
forced to buy it anew, without any regard being had
to the money that has been already paid ; and it is
not even certain that I shall be permitted to buy it
again. I never heard of such a thing! God will put
His hand to it, and take care of a poor persecuted
creature."

" They have done what they projected," writes she
on the 21st of October. " The Commissioners have
been here taking an estimate of everything in and out
of the house, and they have given orders to all my

tenants to pay me no more rent. The cause of this is my having made my composition with the Parliaments that Cromwell called. This injustice has no sooner been executed than the leaders of the army have broken up the Parliament, who thought they had entire power over them. They have chosen Mr. Fleetwood for their head. What Government they will establish is not yet known. The changes are so sudden, and every thing is so uncertain that it is very difficult to form any judgment about the future. They assure me my affairs will improve presently. May God watch over them, and turn everything to His glory, and to the good of those who put their trust in Him."

Another change, and a more serious one than the oscillations of power between the various shades of the Revolutionary party, was silently approaching. For several years the position of General Monk had been quietly growing in importance. He had been a faithful, but not an enthusiastic, adherent of the Long Parliament and of Cromwell, and, since the death of the Protector, he had kept himself secluded in his government of Scotland, taking no part in any intrigue, and not committing himself to any party.

His prudent course had attracted the attention of all thinking people. Politicians of every party paid court to him, but he was impenetrable and cold to all.

He had been on the point of declaring himself at the insurrection of July, but on the defeat of Sir George Booth he resumed his reserve. When Lambert drove out the Parliament, Monk openly sided with the civil power, from which he held his own appointment.

"You have seen how the Parliament has been broken up by the army," wrote Lady Derby, on the 2nd of December, 1659. "General Monk, who commands the army in Scotland, has since that opposed himself to the army by a declaration, and has seized Berwick, a sufficiently strong town on the frontier, it is said, where he is now negotiating some kind of treaty with Lambert; but people say they find it hard to agree. Monk has written to the City of London, which, report says, is divided. The governing body at present consists of twenty-three persons, mostly officers of the army, and one lawyer. God in His goodness will bring out order from our disorder.

"As to my personal affairs, I have been allowed to receive my rents, on giving other security jointly with my own; but only with much difficulty."

Monk's negotiations with Lambert came to nothing, and he took the road to London, without having declared himself, protesting that he was devoted to the Parliament. Fairfax, who had just raised the County of York in the same cause, supported him. At Cold-

stream Monk learnt that the English army, alarmed
by his progress, and weakened by internal dissensions,
had recalled the Long Parliament. Almost at the
same time he received the formal thanks of the restored
Parliament, but without any invitation to come to
London. He nevertheless continued his march, not,
however, allowing his plans to transpire. On the
11th of February he led his troops into the City, and
announced to the Lord Mayor that he had come to
take up his head-quarters there. " I have written this
morning to the Parliament," said he, " to request that
they will issue orders in a week for the elections to
take place that will fill the vacant seats, and that they
will dissolve on the 6th of May, to give place to a free
and complete Parliament. I have resolved, meanwhile,
to remain with my army amongst you until I have seen
my letter obeyed, and the wishes of the City and of
the nation accomplished." A week after, on the 20th
of February, Monk himself caused all the members
excluded in 1648 to return to the House ; and on the
16th of March the Long Parliament, for twenty years
the real sovereigns of England, voted its own dissolution and the opening of the new Parliament on the
25th of April.

Monk had now decided on his course. In reply
to a letter which Sir John Grenville brought to him

from the King, he wrote on the 20th of March, demanding in return for his services a general amnesty, with the exception, at the most, of four persons ; the recognition of the sales of confiscated property ; and liberty of conscience for all his subjects.

All over the country the Royalist reaction burst out spontaneous and ungovernable. Those who were persecuted yesterday became the persecutors of to-day, recovering, weapon in hand, the houses and lands which had been taken from them, and at the same time seizing the horses and furniture which they found there. Cromwell's widow fled from London. Everywhere the Revolutionary party were struck with the same terror with which they had so long inspired their adversaries. The self-imposed Government of the country had not yet spoken; but the excitement of the people, bursting the bounds of moderation and prudence which Monk and the Parliament would have imposed, declared itself on every side.

On the 1st of May, Sir John Grenville presented himself at the door of the House of Commons, and was immediately admitted.

"Mr. Speaker," said he, "I am ordered by the King, my master, to hand you this letter, in order that you may read it to the House."

The letter was dated from Breda, "the twelfth

year of our reign," and was addressed to "our trusty
and well-beloved the Speaker of the House of Commons." While the House, standing with uncovered
heads, listened to the King's letter and the declaration
of his political intentions, Grenville carried the message
for the Lords to their House, where he was received
by the forty-one peers present, who came with the
Chancellor to meet him ; and the thanks of the House
for the gracious message he had brought from the
King were immediately given him. The same day
the whole Parliament, at the suggestion of the Lords,
declared that, "according to the fundamental laws of
the kingdom, the Government resides, and ought to
reside, in the King, Lords, and Commons."

On the 7th of May the Countess writes thus :—

" My letter of the 12th of last month " (which is
lost) " would tell you of the hope we had of the
restoration of the King. This one will tell you that, by
the grace of God, the Parliament has done justice, and
recognized his Majesty. On the 1st of this month the
Houses of Lords and Commons unanimously consented to it. All are delighted, and have given evidence of their repentance for their past conduct. This
change is so great, I can hardly believe it. The King
has written three letters,—to the two Houses, and to
General Monk, who has conducted this affair with a

prudence that will cause him to be esteemed for all generations. It is true that this passes human wisdom, and that in all humility we ought to recognize in it the hand of the Eternal; it is beyond our understanding, and can never be enough admired. Neither can it be believed, except by those who have seen all that has happened during the past year. Lambert, after escaping from the Tower, tried to carry out his bad designs, which were at once defeated. He has now been again consigned to the same prison, but he is more strongly guarded.

" My son Derby has taken his place in the House of Peers, according to his rank. His younger brother has been elected to the other House, but with much opposition; however, by the grace of God, he was successful. My second son is with the King, his master, who, they tell me, does him the honour of liking him; and I have the hope of seeing him soon, if I can, please God, make preparation for going to London. I should be already there if I could have found the means of accomplishing it, but my poverty is very great; yet I must make an effort, for the good of my children depends on it.

" You may believe that the sight of the great world and the joy therein will call up many and opposite thoughts, and the contemplation of my own mis-

fortunes in the midst of so much happiness will revive
very bitter recollections.

"Forgive me, dear sister, if I occupy you so long
with subjects so little pleasant; but the knowledge
that you do me the honour to be interested in all that
concerns me, makes me take this liberty. I will not,
however, trespass longer on your patience, and will
only assure you that no one can be more devoted to
you than I,—who can never be anything else to my
dear sister than her very humble and very obedient
sister, and very faithful servant."

The work of pacification was not yet completed.
Not only did numerous delicate questions remain un-
settled, but doubts and uncertainties of various kinds
arose in the minds of many good people. Already the
general amnesty which the country had been allowed
to hope for seemed to be limited. The Bills intended
to secure religious liberty, and to confirm the sale of
confiscated property, remained suspended, impeded in
their course by the Cavaliers.

The King was at Breda, waiting for the Commissioners of the Parliament. Crowds of visitors flocked
to him every day. "Cavaliers, Presbyterians, Repub-
licans, Cromwellians came in their own interests to
boast of their fidelity, or to excuse their errors; to
recall their past services, or promise new ones; and

to seek their rewards, whether already earned or by anticipation. When Grenville arrived, bearing the gift voted by the House of Commons, with 30,000*l.* in gold and in letters of change, the happy King sent for the Princess of Orange and the Duke of York, that they might see this treasure, to which their eyes had long been so little accustomed, before it was taken out of the valise of the messenger."*

The Commissioners from the two Houses at length arrived, and with them came the Presbyterian ministers, who obtained from the King nothing but vague promises of personal liberty, without any concessions on the subject of the ceremonies of the Church of England.

The English fleet, in command of Admiral Montagu, had just cast anchor in the Bay of Schevelengen, in sight of the Hague, and Charles was urged to take possession of his throne. After taking leave of the States-General, and thanking them for their magnificent hospitality, he recommended his sister, the Princess of Orange, and Prince William, his nephew, to Jean de Witt, Pensioner of Holland, assuring the States that he would be as grateful for evidences of their good affection shown to them as if he should receive it in his own person. Jean de Witt replied,

* M. Guizot, *Protectorate of Richard Cromwell.*

in the name of the States of Holland, by a "discourse which exceeded in respectful and friendly professions all that had been hitherto said to the King by the Dutch authorities. As politic as he was wise, the Dutch patrician, who contended in Holland against the House of Orange, desired to be at peace with England, whatever might be the Government of that country, and sought with some anxiety the friendship of her new master."*

On the 23rd of May, 1660, the King embarked at the Hague, on board a vessel which had hitherto been called the *Naseby*, but to which he now gave the name of the *Royal Charles*, and landed at noon on the 25th at Dover, where Monk awaited him, surrounded by an immense crowd. On the 29th he entered London, after receiving at Blackheath the address of the army, which was submissive, but cold. In London, the satisfaction was animated and hearty. "I stood in the Strand," writes Evelyn in his Journal, "and beheld it, and blessed God. All this was done without one drop of blood shed, and by that very army which rebelled against him. But it was the Lord's doing, for such a restoration was never mentioned in any history, ancient or modern, since the return of the Jews from the Babylonish Captivity."

* M. Guizot, *Protectorate of Richard Cromwell.*

The King himself expressed some ironical surprise at this satisfaction. "It is certainly a mistake," said he, "that I did not come back sooner, for I have not met any one to-day who has not professed to have always desired my return."

CHAPTER X.

LIFE AT COURT.

" OUR good news is so public that I have no doubt you know it," wrote Lady Derby on the 26th of May. " We may well say God has done wonders, for which may His name be for ever blessed." The Countess was then about to start for London, whence she wrote, on the 16th of July :—

" I have been here for six weeks, and the King has done me the honour to treat me with great kindness and sympathy in my heavy afflictions. Nothing, however, has yet been done for me. Such confusion prevails in the Court and in public affairs that it would require much more cleverness than I possess to see my way through all this disorder. The King is overwhelmed with business, and has promoted some who have not hitherto done him good service, and cannot, it seems to me, ever be of much use to him : I am sure it is against his own inclination, but his advisers think it is good policy to govern in this fashion. I hope that, after working so many miracles to bring his Majesty back to us, God will strengthen his throne and give him grace to re-establish his church, and deliver it from schism, of which it is now so full. For the last week the Marquis of Argyle has been, with several others, a prisoner in the Tower, which shows us the vanity of this world. He has had his day, and in the end he will receive the punishment which he so justly merits.

"I am engaged, dear sister, in pursuing the pretended judges of Monsieur, my late husband, and I hope to have justice on them, which I do not desire so much for my own satisfaction as to draw God's blessing on the King and his people, by the punishment of those who spilt that dear and innocent blood with so much cruelty. I have already made some progress in the matter, and I hope to-morrow to have the issue as I desire it. I leave all to God, and I shall at least have the consolation of having done my duty. Many who have undergone similar losses have followed my example."

Strange blindness of human passion! This true Christian hopes to draw the blessing of Heaven upon the King and the people by pursuing an act of personal

vengeance, not less at variance with the amnesty proclaimed by the King than with the words of pardon
pronounced by Lord Derby upon the scaffold :—" Forgive me as I have forgiven them."

Soon after the restoration of Charles to the throne
of England, Louis XIV. terminated the wars that
had so long desolated Europe, by the treaty of the
Pyrenees and his marriage with the Infanta Maria
Theresa of Spain, who had just arrived in Paris when
Lady Derby wrote on the 13th of August :

" If your young Queen resembles the Queen her
mother-in-law, and if she has the advantage of com-
plexion, she cannot but be a very charming person ;
she seemed to me very beautiful. It is thought our
Queen will not come this winter, fearing the climate,
which is not good for delicate lungs. The Princess
Royal " (Princess of Orange) " is preparing for the
journey. The gentlemen of the States, to whom she
has recommended her son, have been informed of it ;
and she has offered to help them with the King, her
brother. Thus we shall have a court of ladies, which
will be a great comfort in enabling us to speak to the
King, who always treats me as I would desire.

" I shall be very glad if M. de Ruvigny comes ; I
was acquainted with him before, but I did not know
he was so much attached to you, and I will do as you

wish. Some people have hoped that Monsieur, your
brother," (the Duc de Bouillon), " would come to renew
the alliance. Monsieur, your father, held the same
office under King James : Monsieur, my brother,
accompanied him on this journey."

" The Princess Royal is expected with the first fair
wind," she wrote on the 12th of September. " The
Duke of York has gone to receive her, and has ordered
my youngest son to follow him ; the one who has the
honour to be known to you has remained with his
Majesty, who does him the honour to like him. Parliament should be adjourned, but there is so much
business, that they have prolonged their sittings from
day to day. The army ought to be entirely disbanded
(a great business) which will surely be accomplished,
and then we shall be able to judge what we are to do.
Everything seems to me in great confusion. May
it please God in his goodness to give wisdom for the
re-establishment of his church, and the prosperity of
the King and his people !

" The Duke of Gloucester has been ill with small-
pox, but by the grace of God, the worst is over. He
is a Prince of great promise. . . . ."

"We lost his Highness, the Duke of Gloucester,
yesterday," adds she on the 17th, " after all the doctors
had judged him out of danger, from the small-pox.

It is a great loss ; the Prince had a mind that cannot
be too highly valued.   May God turn this affliction to
our amendment."

Things fell out as the Countess had anticipated.
She writes on 4th of October : " The army is disbanded, but with much difficulty.   I hope, with God's
blessing, all will go well."

The King had resolved to get rid of the sombre
faces which had produced so uncomfortable an im-
pression upon him on the day of his entrance into
London ; and Monk offered no resistance to this
measure, which stripped him of all power.   The discontent was extreme, and various plans had been
formed for assassinating the General.   The soldiers
were not all disbanded when an insurrection broke
out in London, headed by Venner, a Fifth Monarchy
man, who went out in the night with about fifty enthu-
siasts, crying, " The sword of the Lord and of Gideon !"
They made a most heroic resistance ; and the regiment
of Guards* which was called out to repel them behaved
so well on the occasion that their conduct furnished
a pretext for retaining them, although Monk would not
make the demand.

---

* This is the regiment of Coldstream Guards, so named in
memory of Monk's entrance into England by Coldstream ; it became
the germ of the standing army.

"We have had a great alarm to-night," wrote Lady Derby on the 7th of January, 1661. "The Anabaptists and other of these discontented sects rose last night, and possessed themselves of some of the gates of St. Paul's Church; but, thank God, all is quiet now : the King's Guards and the London Militia repelled the fanatics, as they are called. Some were killed, and others wounded. The Mayor has testified his zeal and his diligence, as well as much spirit, in suppressing these disorders. His Royal Highness " (the Duke of York—the King was absent) " had given his orders beforehand; but he never left Whitehall ; and he was right."

And on the 11th of January she wrote : "These fanatics are to be tried to-morrow. They have confessed their designs, which are the most odious imaginable. They call themselves Fifth Monarchy men, and consider our Saviour Jesus Christ their King, and the author of all their crimes; and a thousand blasphemies of this nature. It is thought that Lambert and Vane have had some share in their schemes, from which may God, in His goodness, preserve the King."

The fanatics were executed immediately; Lambert and Vane were not sentenced till the following year ; and Vane alone was destined to perish on the scaffold. A sad ending for a man of such remarkable character

and so much elevation of mind! Though a visionary,
he was a sincere and fervent Christian, whose indomitable devotion to his theories was unshaken by even
the prospect of martyrdom.

A curious and amusing change appears now in
the correspondence of Lady Derby, as well as in the
subjects which engaged her attention. After more
than thirty years passed in the country, away from
courts; after severe afflictions and acts of rare heroism,
the spirit of the "grande dame" suddenly re-awakens
in Charlotte de la Trémoille. The atmosphere of the
Court resumes its influence over her. The movements
of the King and the Queen, their little favours, their
good graces, the marriage of the King, the affairs of
the Duke and Duchess of York, the Countess's ex-
pectations of personal advancement at the Court, all
assume supreme importance in the eyes of the widow,
who had lost her husband, her fortune, her position;
whose life for ten years had been passed in sorrow
and privations, and whose only wish had been to die.

" The Princess Royal arrived yesterday," wrote
she, on the 22nd of September. " She was on the
sea when she learnt her bitter loss, which is one of
the greatest the King and his people could sustain;
and we all individually feel it deeply, for the Prince
honoured my two youngest sons with his liking. He

had very remarkable qualities, which would have rendered him one of the greatest men of the age.

"I hear nothing of the King thinking of marrying
a woman of an opposite religion. All his most important advisers say it would be his ruin. They speak
of the Princess of Denmark ; but, in my belief, there
is nothing that the King has yet thought seriously
about. May God put into his Majesty's heart
what will be best for his peace and his glory. If
he thinks of riches, he could not have more than with
Mademoiselle " (de Montpensier; the great Mademoiselle) : "which I would wish with all my heart ;
but I fear that, having been despised in his poverty,
he would be unlikely now to contemplate such a
match. M. de Ruvigny has been twice to see me,
but I had gone to visit the Princess, who has received
me very kindly, and my daughter Strafford with much
feeling. The two others will go to her to-morrow. . . ."

"No proposal has been made for the Infanta of
Portugal ; everybody is desirous that the King should
marry (but I see no appearance of it), and above all
that he should marry a Protestant. It is said that
many wish Mdlle. d'Orange, but I do not know if
this is true. I hear her figure is fine, and not at
all spoiled. Prince Rupert has been here for two
days, and lodges in the apartment of his late Royal

Highness. The Princess, his sister, occupies that of the Queen, her mother, who, they say, has borne the loss of the Prince with great fortitude.

"I beg you will tell me what you think of our young Princess" (the Princess Henrietta), "who, they say, is to marry Monsieur, although many wanted her to have the Emperor. . . ."

"I went yesterday to present myself to the Princess," she writes on the 8th of October, "but the King was only a minute with her. She told me that the Queen, her mother, is to come as soon as possible, and before the marriage of the Princess Henrietta, whom she will bring with her. Everyone tries to guess the reason of this sudden change; for, two days before, it was said she would not come till spring, and that she was afraid of the winter air of this country, which is injurious to delicate lungs. People think that Prince Rupert has brought proposals for the marriage of the Emperor and the Princess. Others say" (in cypher) "that the daughter of the Chancellor is *enceinte* by the Duke, the uncle of the young Prince of Orange. *She* says there is a contract : *he* denies it absolutely. The Queen, who does not like the Chancellor, is coming to work his downfall. Everyone hates him."

Edward Hyde, afterwards Earl of Clarendon, had,

in fact, made nearly all the courtiers his enemies. He
had been the most faithful as well as the most able
of the counsellors of both father and son, in good and
in bad fortune. Before the Restoration he had steadily
opposed the Presbyterians, who regarded him as too
much attached to the English Church, and he was
not more acceptable to the dissolute and unprincipled
of the Court party, who dreaded his austere demeanour
and his high principles. The King, however, had
always remained faithful to him, in spite of the
annoyance which the Chancellor's remonstrances often
occasioned him. But the secret marriage of his brother,
the Duke of York, with Anne Hyde, the Earl of
Clarendon's daughter, endangered more seriously the
father's favour at Court. He felt, or pretended to
feel, so much anger that he asked the King to put
the bride in the Tower, and, on the rather ironical
refusal of his Majesty, he himself imprisoned his
daughter in her apartment. The Duke of York for
several days denied the marriage, but the birth of
a daughter reconciled him to the wife whom he had
allowed to be calumniated.

"In her father's house the girl is called Duchess,"
wrote Lady Derby on the 30th of October; "but
everything is put off till the coming of the Queen."

"I have to beg you a thousand pardons," writes

she, a few days later, " for not having told you before
of the arrival of the Queen, which took place last
Friday, to everybody's delight, with the acclamations
of the whole nation. I saw her on her arrival, and
kissed her hand. She met me with much emotion,
and received me with tears and great kindness. You
may imagine what I felt. Her Majesty charms all
who see her, and her courtesy cannot be enough
praised. She has constantly received visitors since
she came, without having kept her room. Our young
Princess is all you said she was."

What an interview must that have been between
the two widows, both French, and both brought to
England to undergo the severest afflictions of life!
Henrietta Maria's natural frivolity had cut her off
from the highest happiness of conjugal life; but the
Countess of Derby had enjoyed it all, and had lost
it for the husband and the son of that Queen whom,
by a miracle, after more than a dozen years of separation, she again met.

Honours now rained on the Countess, though she
had to wait long for more substantial benefits.

" I told you about my illness," wrote she, on the
3rd of December, to her sister-in law. " I can tell you
now that I am better, thank God! But it is not so
much for that I trouble you, as to tell you the surprise

I had last night. I had only my daughter Strafford with me, when suddenly they told me the King was on the stairs, attended only by the Marquis of Ormond. He did me the honour to assure me that he wished to take charge of my children and me, and he told me that that little matter was done which I spoke to you about; and that it was his own business which had prevented him from doing me this honour before. It must be owned that he is the most charming prince in the world! I have not been to Court for a week or ten days, but I am going after dinner."

The King had paid the Countess a visit. This—in return for twenty years of affliction, the loss of all her property, and the death of her husband! Was he not truly " the most charming prince in the world ? "

Events followed one another rapidly at Court. The Countess, who was silent during the siege of Latham and in the Isle of Man, has always something to tell her sister-in-law. Now it is a death and now a marriage.

" My last told you of the illness of the Princess Royal," she wrote, on the 24th of December, " and now, with much grief, I have to tell you she is at the point of death, and I fear she may have passed away by this time. Good people will be glad to know that on the third day of her illness, feeling some weakness

that the doctor said was occasioned by sea-sickness, she
asked for a cordial, in order that she might have more
strength to receive the sacrament, of which she partook
with great devotion, and perfect confidence in her
salvation; and when the King burst into tears, she
spoke of death without fear or emotion. She recommended to him her son, for whose sake alone she
wished for life, if it was God's will. And, the cordial
having given her a little strength, she desired to make
her will, which she did with great patience and in a
very Christian spirit. This was on Friday at five
o'clock in the morning; she was better on Saturday,
and on Sunday they thought her out of danger.
The Queen has not seen her since Wednesday, which
made me sure she was out of danger; but what induced
me to believe the contrary is that the doctors have
never agreed as to whether it was measles or small-pox.
Her women and others tell me that bleeding her three
times so reduced her that her Royal Highness had not
strength enough to throw out the virulence of the disorder. The Queen, her mother, selected the doctors
who were to attend her, and who were her own—
Mr. Colloden and Dr. Fraser; the latter was formerly
in France about the King's person, and is in some
disgrace with his Majesty.

"The Queen, his mother, is very much vexed that

the marriage of the Duke" (of York) " is absolutely
recognized, every one openly paying court to the
Duchess. The King brought about the reconciliation,
carrying the Duke, his brother, to Madame, his wife.
I pray God that He will give His blessing to this
marriage, and grace to us to humble ourselves under
our chastisements, which seem to me very grievous,
for, in truth, our Princess was an excellent person : all
the good and rare qualities she possessed were natural
endowments, for she had had her own way from childhood, those about her having thought more of their own
interests than of what was good for her, or proper for her
position.

" I had a thousand things to tell you that I cannot
write. I do not know if this affliction will accelerate
or retard the Queen's journey. The Princess "
(Henrietta) "changed her lodging from Whitehall to
St. James's, where she is at present, and was very well
yesterday. All these losses in the Royal family grieve
and shock their friends. May it please God to withdraw His hand, and preserve those who remain to us,
and protect the King and guide him through all
dangers. That which threatened his safety has been
discovered, and every day people concerned in the
conspiracy are arrested. . . . . The Princess died at
noon, and, when she was not in convulsions, was quite

sensible. I have just come from visiting the Queen,
who is much distressed. I saw her. May God withdraw His judgments from us!"

After this death come the Court reconciliations.

" I thought of writing to you, dear sister, on
Thursday, the day after the departure of the Queen,
and of our adorable Princess, but I was so tired with
having been to Court, which is always attended with
inconvenience to people of my age, that I could not
indulge in that pleasure, and tell you of the reconciliation of the Queen and the Duchess, which took place
the evening before the departure of her Majesty.
There was a great crowd, and so much noise that one
could only see their actions ; as for their words, it was
impossible to hear them : those of the Duchess were
very humble ; she knelt on both knees, and then the
Queen, kissed her, and afterwards the Princess, and
they saluted one another. I am sure she will describe
it all to mademoiselle your daughter, whom she greatly
likes. The Queen immediately directed the Princess
to retire, for she feared that in so great a crowd there
might be danger from small-pox ; but I think it was
for some other reason that her Majesty led the Duchess
from her bed-chamber to the ante-room, where she
made her and the Duke of York sit down. They say
that the next day the Queen was kinder to Madame

her daughter-in-law than the night before. In short, it has gone off very well, and her Majesty has managed well in the matter of the arrangement she desired.[*]

" The King says she will return soon, though I doubt it. He has gone to take her to Portsmouth ; but the Duke, who is not very well, remains here. People are apprehensive about the journey of the King, as it is to a part of the country where he is not liked ; but he has no fear, though he has heard some ugly rumours.

" There is much talk of the marriage with the Infanta of Portugal : great advantages in the Indies, and much wealth here are offered ; as to religion, she is to be under no restraint ; the King will place who- ever she likes about her. An ambassador from Portugal is expected very soon. I only know all this from hearsay. May God in His grace preserve our good King and guide him for His honour and the advancement of His glory. . . . .

" I have a request to make to you, which is, to direct one of your women to buy me the most beautiful doll to be had, that will undress ; it is for a little girl whose parents I greatly wish to oblige,

---

[*] Henrietta Maria always intended to come to England, in order to see all her children together, and to get the matter of her dowry settled.—*Clarendon.*

as they have been attentive to me. Forgive me for this liberty.

"I forgot to tell you that our Princess had a wager with my daughter Strafford, and her Royal Highness has lost; she has done my daughter the honour of promising her a portrait of herself. If mademoiselle your daughter should find an opportunity of reminding her of it, she will oblige her cousin. . . . .

"Every day, as we remember her merits, the loss of our Princess is more and more felt. The King, her brother, has accepted the guardianship of Monsieur her son, according to her desire. His Royal Highness has felt her death more than might have been expected from a child of his age. The Queen his grandmother has taken away with her all the jewels belonging to him, which her Royal Highness had left to him, as coming from the house of Orange. Her Majesty thinks she should take care of them, and that they are safer with her . . . . The grief of princes does not last long; they have so many things to occupy them that they soon forget their sorrows. . . . . Every one has been as much astonished as you have been at the reconciliation of the Queen" (with the Duchess,) "but I believe it is only in appearance, and that it has helped her and many of her servants to get their affairs settled.

"I have given six Jacobuses to la Pierre for his journey, which will pay for the doll; if more is wanted order them to advance it. It is for the Chancellor's grand-daughter."

Eleven regicides had perished on the scaffold, paying with their lives for a crime inspired by the violent passions of the time. But the most important amongst them had hitherto escaped punishment. The accomplices in the King's murder had indeed suffered for their deed, but the leaders of the Revolution were beyond the reach of earthly vengeance. Human wrath, when expended in vain, becomes puerile and contemptible, but executed on a corpse, it is not merely despicable but odious. The Countess of Derby seemed to feel this, in spite of the inextinguishable vengeance that she nourished. She wrote on the 31st of January, 1661,—"There was a fast yesterday in memory of the death of the late King, of glorious memory, which was observed throughout his Majesty's dominions. An Act of Parliament had been passed ordering that the bodies of Cromwell, Ireton, and Bradshaw, should be disinterred the day before, dragged on a hurdle through the town, hanged on the common gibbet" (at Tyburn Gate), "and buried under it. Nothing makes me recognize so clearly the vanity of the world, and that we have no hope but in the fear of God. It will be said with reason that it would have been better for this man if he had never been born! All this wickedness, these murders, this Macchiavellian policy," (Macchiavelli was Cromwell's favourite author,) "have marked him and his family with eternal infamy. The thought that it is better to be poor and be at peace with one's conscience, makes me patiently bear my miserable condition and that of my children ; for though this pension will help me a little to live, yet, having received nothing for them but that, I do not know what will become of us. A great deal is promised, but the fulfilment is long in coming."

Was it, indeed, the body of the great Protector that the King and the two Houses of Parliament had thus exposed to outrage ? Strange rumours were current even then, which may now be read in the *Harleian Miscellany*. The story ran that, as a protection against a revolution in human affairs which might disturb the repose of his remains, Cromwell, by his own order, had been secretly interred on the battle-field of Naseby, the scene of his great and decisive victory over Charles I. ; and that, by a subtle precaution, which cruelly defeated itself, the embalmed body of King Charles had been substituted for that of Oliver Cromwell in the coffin bearing his name, which was deposited in Henry VII.'s Chapel at Westminster.

It is added that, when the body was hung on the gibbet at Tyburn, and Royalists went to feast their eyes on the dreadful spectacle, they perceived with horror that the corpse bore traces of decapitation, and they even thought they recognized in its disfigured face the features of the King. However this might be, the immediate interment of the body was ordered.

This strange story, improbable though it sounds, confirms a statement made by Clarendon himself, to the effect that, at the Restoration almost all the witnesses of the burial of King Charles I. were dead, and that those who survived found their memories so confused by the alterations made in the Chapel at Windsor, that the exact spot in which the body of the King had been placed could never be positively ascertained, so that, necessarily, all idea of removing it, or of performing any funeral ceremony, had to be relinquished.

Charles II.'s marriage was still pending ; but his own thoughts and leisure were occupied with other matters.

" They say the King's marriage with the Infanta is broken off," writes Lady Derby, on the 14th of February, 1661. " An Italian alliance is now talked of ; but I do not know who the lady is, and many say the Queen is busying herself with this negotiation. It

is not the Cardinal's niece.* The report is abroad
that the Earl of Bristol is really going on this business, though he says it is on his own private affairs.
Whatever may come of it, I pray God it may be for
His glory and honour, and the advantage of his
Majesty." (In cypher :—) "All the good folks are
greatly shocked to see the King employ so wicked a
person, and one so unfit to represent him at a foreign
Court.

"People here are talking of your great preparations for war, and say it is to be with Venice; but it
is feared there may be an understanding amongst the
Catholics, and that they are brewing mischief against
us. Tell me what you think, and it shall be private."

Court intrigues multiplied. The Spanish ambassador, M. de Wateville, employed every device in his
power to prevent the Portuguese alliance, which was
supported by Louis XIV., for two reasons, as he tells
us in his Memoirs : "the first, to help the Portuguese,
whom I else saw in danger of soon yielding; the
second, to give me more means of assisting them
myself if necessary, notwithstanding the treaty of the
Pyrenees, by which I am forbidden to do so."

* The marriage of Charles II. with one of the nieces of Cardinal
Mazarin, had been on the tapis at the time of Sir George Booth's
insurrection. When this was put down the Cardinal retired.

"The King's marriage is still talked of," says Lady Derby, on the 17th of February; "and M. de Bristol is gone about it. There are so many different reports that one cannot tell what to believe. May God give him a Queen who will be agreeable to him, and a blessing to his Majesty and his people. I think he will make as good a husband as his Royal Highness; and there never was such an one as he is. He even surpasses the King his father. You may judge of the rest.

"Where you are nothing is talked of but marriages, and here nothing but the King's coronation, which is to take place on the 23rd of April. Those who have the means are making preparations for great display. We are not of this number. The Knights of the Garter will be installed two or three days before. They have discovered the name of a member of the House of Duras-Gaillard, Seigneur de Duras. I hope yet to find out the year in which he entered the order. The description you sent me of their arms has not been understood, for you say nothing of the field or of the posture of the lions. I should think that, knowing the name, they will be able to find the rest in their genealogies. I believe it was when the English possessed Guienne. I am sorry to be of so little use to my relations, for there is no one who desires more to be of service to them."*

And on the 25th she adds :—

" They say M. de Bristol is to bring back a Queen to us, one of the daughters or sisters of the Duc de Mantone. For the present it is a great secret. The Parliament of Scotland has declared the Covenant to be criminal, and opposed to the divine right and authority of his Majesty. And on these heads they are proceeding with the trial of the Duke of Argyle, who, it is believed, will suffer as he deserves; for I think he is one of the most wicked men in the world, and that he has committed unheard-of cruelties.

" Plays are often acted at Court, and the King and their Royal Highnesses have been present at two this evening, at the Duchess of Buckingham's. It is not usual, in the absence of one's husband, to take part in such gaieties. Her sister-in-law has declared herself a Catholic ; she has never had much religion, so it is no great loss. May God in His goodness support the true faith in this kingdom, which is oppressed on all sides !

" Prince Maurice of Nassau will soon be here. I have heard nothing upon the subject of his embassy, but it is supposed to relate to the Prince of Orange,

The Duras were allied to the Bouillons.

to whom the King is guardian." (The embassy of Prince Maurice concerned Charles II.'s marriage, rather than his guardianship of the young Prince William.)

Lady Derby, on the 14th of March, wrote in cypher to her sister-in-law :—

" I greatly desire the marriage of Mademoiselle, but the King has an aversion to it on account of the contempt she has shown for him Since the coming of Prince Maurice, people speak a great deal of Mdlle. d'Orange. The Spanish Ambassador takes that side, in order to oppose Portugal. Nothing now will content this people but a Protestant marriage. It seems to me that the Chancellor ought to desire Mademoiselle more than any one else. Would to God I could serve her ! it would be with all my heart. I have spoken of her to the Marquis of Ormond, but I meet with small encouragement. If I knew whom the Queen favours, I could act to more purpose. I thought Mademoiselle was to marry the son of the Florentine." She adds in ordinary writing :—" At last you have lost M. le Cardinal; every one is wondering what will happen next. They say that Monsieur your brother is to be one of the first ministers of the State. I am sure he will use his power for the benefit of good people."

The Countess of Derby continued to be on bad terms with her eldest son. In right of her marriage settlement she possessed the estate of Knowsley, in Lancashire. She writes to her sister-in-law :—"The Isle of Man was restored to my son Derby immediately after the arrival of the King. Monsieur his late father gave it to me for twenty-one years; and my son, without saying a word to me, after I had helped him in prison, and maintained him and all his family, has treated me in this manner! Our friends advise me strongly to come to some agreement by which I should have half the revenue. But I do not believe I shall get anything, except by force. His wife is a person without a single good quality. What shocks me most of all in her is, that she never speaks the truth, and that she makes her husband do things that are quite unworthy of him, which, however, I fear, he is too much inclined to do ; and I apprehend there will be complaints of him from the Parliament, for not acting legally in his government of the provinces of Lancashire and Chester, having raised money and overtaxed the people; but I cannot help it, as I am quite a stranger to his proceedings. . . . .
As for that sword which has been restored to my son, I cannot tell what it means ; for Monsieur his father never had any carried before him in the Isle

of Man. It is a piece of his wife's vanity to have it put in the *Gazette*."

The Earl of Derby had never made a display of those insignia of royalty to which the possession of the Isle of Man entitled him, and he had advised his son to follow his example, having written in his last instructions to him;—" Some might think it a mark of grandeur that the lords of this island have been called kings, and I might be of that opinion if I knew how this country could maintain itself independent of other nations, and that I had no interest in another place. But herein I agree with your and my great and wise ancestor, Thomas, second Earl of Derby, and with him conceive, that to be a great lord is more honourable than to be a petty king.

" Besides, it is not for a King to be subject to any but the King of kings, nor doth it please a King that any of his subjects should affect that title, were it but to act it in a play ; witness the scruples raised, and objections made, by my enemies in his Majesty's council, of my being too near allied to Royalty to be trusted with too great power, whose jealousies and vile suggestions have proved of very ill consequence to his Majesty's interests and my service of him. There never was a wise subject that would willingly offend his King ; but if offence were given from the Prince, would rather humble himself before him as the only means to recover his favour, without which no subject can propose to live with honour or glory.

" To complete this counsel, take it for granted that it is your honour to give honour to your sovereign ; it is safe and comfortable ; therefore, in all your actions let it visibly appear in this Isle ; let him be prayed for duly ; let all writings and oaths of officers and soldiers, &c., &c., have relation of allegiance to him." *

The Countess was actuated by the same modesty and unswerving fidelity which had governed her husband's conduct. She readily forgot the King's wrongs and offences to herself ; and when she was once more at Court she felt in her natural element.

" A lady who thinks she knows the news has just told me the Queen is coming back to London," she writes to her sister-in-law in the month of March, " and I am advised to entreat you, and all those to whom I have the honour of belonging, to ask her Majesty to do me the honour of making me one of the ladies of her bed-chamber. M. de Ruvigny knows what M. de St. Albans said to him on this subject. If the proposal is made in the right way, I think it will succeed. It would give me the opportunity of talking to the King,

* SEACOME'S *House of Stanley.*

of serving my friends, and advancing my children ; and I should be able to retire when I liked. Think about it, dear sister, whose I am entirely."

And on the 8th of April following, she wrote :—

"His Majesty is going to Windsor in a week to install the Knights of the Garter, who were created while the King was in exile. He has created four within the last week, of whom my son-in-law, the Earl of Strafford, is one. They are still talking of the marriage with the Infanta of Portugal." And then (in cypher), " I have learnt that the Portuguese marriage is not yet arranged. I have had Mademoiselle proposed, and I have some hopes, provided they are sure of the religion. May God give us a Queen who will be a blessing to the King and the people. All over the country they are electing persons friendly to the King's service, who desire the good of the people. Thank God they have not followed the example of London, where they have returned men who, it is believed, will not be admitted into Parliament." *

The King's coronation had been delayed for several months. It took place at length on the 23rd of April, 1661. The Countess of Derby thus describes it to her sister-in-law.

---

* The elections of the City of London had been hostile to candidates of the Church of England.

" I did not write to you by the last post, as it was
the day on which the King was to make a kind of
entry into London. He went from the Tower to
Whitehall on horseback, with all the peers of the realm,
a most magnificent sight, and his Majesty looked very
noble. His good looks and his courtesy are beyond
description. The Duke of Northumberland was Lord
High Constable, and the Duke of Ormond Lord High
Steward on this occasion ; the latter is always of his
Majesty's household. The day before yesterday was
the day of the coronation, which is a most august
ceremony. The Bishop of Worcester preached the
sermon, which was excellent, and showed us our
duty, not forgetting that of the King. His text
was from Proverbs,—" May God enable us to follow
what he has taught us." M. Brevient knows this
person, and can tell you how good his life is, and how
orthodox his doctrine. The Archbishop of Canterbury
placed the crown on his Majesty's head, and was
assisted by the Bishop of London, on account of the
Archbishop's great age. The ceremony was long, and
I saw both it and the dinner, without any inconvenience,
with the Duchess of York. I have no doubt it will be
all published. The most curious part of the ceremony
was when the Lord High Constable, the Earl Marshal,
and the Lord High Steward, came on horseback into

the hall, the Lord High Constable carrying a dish—
and remaining so all dinner time; after which two of
them went away, and the Lord High Constable only
remained; then the two returned, bringing with them
the King's Champion all in armour, with his spear and
target carried before him, to the sound of trumpets and
drum, and at the same time the heralds proclaimed the
King sovereign of these kingdoms, not forgetting that
of France; and then the Champion threw down his
gauntlet, saying if any one denied it he was there to
maintain it with his sword.

"The King and the Duke of York dined at one
large table, and the lords at another in the great hall,
and the mayor, the judges, and the sheriffs at a third.
All this ceremony lasted seven or eight hours; and
it was a very grand and imposing sight, the lords
in the robes proper for the occasion, which are very
becoming. It is the last thing of the kind I shall see;
and I have greatly desired to witness it, having prayed
with tears to be permitted to behold this crown on the
head of his Majesty. May he and his posterity long
wear it, and may God accord to him and to us the
grace of never forgetting His miraculous blessings."

CHAPTER XI.

LAST LETTERS.

WHILE the Court and the people of London were enjoying the festivities of the coronation, the Marquis of Argyle, who had so lately placed the crown on the King's brow at Scone, was at Edinburgh, awaiting his sentence of death.

"It is thought that Argyle will be condemned in Scotland, where he will be beheaded," wrote the Countess of Derby, on the 30th of May; but at this time Argyle was already dead. Accused of having delivered King Charles I. to the English Parliament, and of having caused the loss of Montrose, he claimed the benefit of the amnesty granted by Charles II. at Stirling; but the charges were numerous, and the most important of them related to events subsequent to the amnesty. He had received 12,000*l.* sterling from

Cromwell, had favoured the invasion of Scotland
by the English, had taken his seat in Richard Cromwell's Parliament, and voted the deposition of the
Stuarts. It was said that throughout he had sought
only the aggrandisement of his own family and the
gratification of his personal ambition, at the expense
of his country and his Sovereign. Argyle defended
himself with ability. His trial lasted four months, and
his fate was still in suspense when the Scotch Parliament were informed of the arrival of a courier from
London. " From the haste of the messenger, who was
accidentally discovered to be of the clan Campbell, it
was believed he brought either a pardon or a respite.
But when the packet was opened, it was found to
contain Argyle's letters to Monk,—a proof of the in-
efficiency of human prudence." * These letters were
full of professions of attachment to the Government
of the Protector, and more than sufficed to take away
his last chance of life. " When solicited to give them
up, Monk wished to wait till they were absolutely
necessary; and then being informed, he says, of what
was required to complete the evidence against the
Duke, he hastened to give them into the hands of
the Parliament. They removed all hesitation. The
next day Argyle was condemned ; and Monk, doubt-

* M. GUIZOT, *Fall of the English Republic.*

less, received the congratulations and the thanks of the
Court with his accustomed humility." *

" I have given him a royal crown," exclaimed
Argyle, when he heard his sentence, "and this is
my reward ! However, he only hastens my course
to a better than his, and he cannot deprive me of
that eternal amnesty of which you will all have
need."

" As I hope to be saved," said he, on mounting the
scaffold, " from my birth to this day I have never had
part, in any manner, either by counsel or by knowledge,
in the death of the late King. And I pray God to
preserve his Majesty, to spread His blessing over him
and his Government, and to give him good and faithful
counsellors." The sentence was executed, and his head
set up on the gate of Edinburgh, replacing that of
Montrose, to whose remains a superb funeral was
given.

" The news came yesterday that Argyle was beheaded, and two more, of the same country " (Guthrie
and Gowan), " were also hanged," wrote Lady Derby
on the 3rd of June. " They all well deserved what
they have suffered ; and we see, from his end, that
the prosperity of the wicked is but for a time."

The Portuguese marriage was at length resolved

* M. GUIZOT, Fall of the English Republic.

on. French policy had counterbalanced that of Spain; and preparations were being made for the reception of the Infanta.

"They say that the fleet is not to set out till the end of this month," wrote Lady Derby on the 3rd of June; "and with a favourable wind it takes three weeks to go there, and as many to return; so that she cannot be here for three months. The Catholics are very strong in her household. M. d'Aubigny is her grand almoner. I do not know how he has been able to get that place, for he stood very well with the Ambassador of Spain, and not so very well with the Chancellor.

"Parliament is going on as usual. They ordered a holiday on the birthday of the King, which is the same day as that of his entrance into London: he has now been back a year. There were sermons in every church, and bonfires at night. This order is to be regarded in future as an Act of Parliament, and this observance is to be always made.

"The Parliament has had the Covenant burnt here as well as in Scotland. Money for the King is to be asked for; they will refuse nothing to his Majesty, although I believe this will be a year of famine, for we have had the strangest weather in the world.

" I have sent my young children to offer a petition
to Parliament representing their miserable condition;
both theirs and mine is to be deplored. And I know
not what will become of me, overwhelmed with debts
as I am. If they would do anything, I would make
up my mind to spend little, and leave the remainder
of what I have to pay my debts."

And on the 20th of June following :—

" The Bishops are recalled to Parliament, where
the Catholics are being discussed. I fear they will
make an oath for them expressly, and that they will
have a great deal of liberty ; it seems to me that everything is tending to that."

The oath, however, was not modified, in spite of
the King's liking for the Catholic religion. The time
for toleration had not yet arrived.

Madame de la Trémoille was deeply occupied with
the marriage of her only daughter, whose religion
had from her birth limited the number of eligible
matches for her in France.

Lady Derby wrote in cypher on the 21st of July:
" I should like to know what you would think of the
Duke of Richmond for the daughter of M. de la
Trémoille. He is the fourth person in England, is
related to the King, and is rich. You saw him in
France before the death of his cousin. Tell me what

she will have on her marriage. He has a daughter by his wife, who was an heiress, and he will have all her property for his life. Doubtless he could aspire to the highest posts at Court."

Mdlle. de la Trémoille was in great favour with the Princess Henrietta.

" I am very glad to learn," writes her aunt, on the 31st July, "that your health allows you to go to Court; it is right that you should do so on account of Mademoiselle your daughter. For many reasons she must keep up the interest that Madame takes in her. Nothing pleases me better than to know that the Princess continues to conduct herself with so much discretion and virtue. You will have heard the conclusion of his Majesty's marriage with the Infanta of Portugal. The King sends over to her a Master of Requests, who speaks Spanish, and knows the language spoken at this Court. It is said that she does not understand French. The Ambassador of the King, her brother, says she is quite a devotee, and had so strong a desire to become a nun that it was very difficult to change her resolution. Some of the Court here are going to drink the waters; and the Duchess of York wishes very much that my daughter Strafford should go with her. It must be confessed that she " (the Duchess) " has a great deal of modesty, and makes much of all persons of virtue; she is passionately attached to his Royal Highness, and he to her. The Liturgy* has not yet been read, but it is hoped that it will be next Sunday. The time of the future Queen's arrival is not yet exactly known. I do not know if the Queen" (Henrietta Maria) "will remain long at Fontainebleau. If she goes to drink the waters of Bourbon she will not be there long. It is still said that she is coming here, and if so she will be much pleased to find that she (the new Queen) is of her religion. May God guide all for his glory."

Lady Derby's interest in the arrival of the two Queens was not unconnected with her hope of obtaining a place at Court. She wrote on the 8th of July :—

"When I told you, dear sister, of my desire to be with the Queen, it was thought that her Majesty's return was certain, and the King's marriage was not at all so. I have a project, which I will tell you of if it succeeds. The Portuguese ambassador is gone. A French tailor has been sent to make dresses for the Queen that is to be, the King not finding those she wears to his taste. For my part, I think the old Spanish dress was much more becoming than what is

* The Prayer book, newly revised, had undergone some modifications.

now worn. The King has been to the Parliament, and passed two Bills, one an Act of benevolence, and the other a general pardon. I thought the Chancellor would have been unable to be present He was not well yesterday, after having been bled ; but that did not prevent his being there.

" The Queen of Bohemia continues very well, and still able to keep about. Rumour says that Monsieur is very jealous of Madame, and that he makes her a very bad husband, which I cannot believe. The Duke of York is very much the reverse ; there never was his equal, he and his wife being inseparable."

And on the 9th of September :—

" I went the other day to the Queen of Bohemia. She has plays performed at her house, and never misses one, being of as youthful a disposition as if she were a girl of twenty. She tells me that she has been informed that the eldest of the Dukes of Limbourg has gone to France with a great retinue, and that he intends to pay his addresses to Mademoiselle your daughter. They say he would be a great match, only that he is married to his cousin-german, who refuses to live with him. His theological advisers, indeed, assure him that he can obtain a divorce ; but I do not approve of this proceeding. I thought it well to let you know of this ; and also that [the King has promised to give me the appointment of governess to his children]" (these words are in cypher), " an important place, which will enable me to confer favours, and do much good. . . . . Yesterday, we had the English Liturgy read in French in the chapel which his Majesty has given them" (the French Protestants?) " We had two excellent sermons, from M. Duret in the morning, and from M. Le Conte in the afternoon. The Duke and Duchess of Ormond were there in the morning, and many others, who came away highly pleased."

The Earl of Sandwich, at the head of a numerous fleet, had just cleared the Mediterranean of the pirates which infested it, and taken possession of Tangier, which had been ceded to England by the Portuguese, on the occasion of the marriage. The Spanish ambassador, furious at the failure of his manœuvres, resolved to revive, at the Court of Charles II., the ancient pretensions of Spain to take precedence of all other crowns. On the day when the Danish minister, M. de Brahe, entered London, a skirmish took place in the streets between the attendants of M. de Wateville, the Spanish ambassador, and those of M. D'Estrades, the ambassador from the Court of France. The bystanders, though taking no part in the dispute, were in favour of the Spaniards. More than fifty

persons were killed or wounded. M. D'Estrades'
coachman was thrown from his seat, the traces of his
horses were cut, and M. de Wateville immediately
drove on before him. This event so enraged
Louis XIV. that M. de Fuensaldagna, the ambassador from Spain to the French Court, was instantly
dismissed thence. Charles II. also took the side of
France in the quarrel.

"I have just been .told that the Spanish ambassador has received orders from the King not to appear
again at Court," wrote Lady Derby ; "and that it is
on account of what passed in the dispute between him
and the French ambassador, he having taken some of
his Majesty's subjects into his pay without his knowledge. They say that the King, his master, does
not sanction his proceedings, which is, perhaps, the
reason why the King" (Charles II.) " has forbidden
him the Court."

Philip IV. did in fact refuse to sanction the course
taken by M. de Wateville ; he recalled him from
London, and promised that in future his ambassadors
should abstain from appearing in ceremonies where
their pretensions might come into collision with the
rights of the French ambassador.

"I do not know that anything more glorious for
France has ever happened since the beginning of the

monarchy," Louis XIV. says in his memoirs : " it is a
kind of homage that leaves no doubt in the minds
even of our enemies, that ours is the first crown of
Christendom. This tumult in London was looked
upon as a misfortune ; it would now be a misfortune if
it had not happened."

Affairs were prospering with both the royal allies ;
Louis XIV. exulted in his superiority over all the
thrones of the earth, and rejoiced in the possession of
a son to inherit this glorious crown. In London
prayers were beginning to be offered for the new
Queen of England, " in the chapel at Whitehall, and
afterwards in all the churches of the kingdom, men-
tioning her by her Christian name." " Both our Queens
cannot be mentioned together," wrote the Countess on
the 14th of November 1661, "and it has been settled
therefore in this way, that her name is to come first in
the prayers."

But Lady Derby was now reduced to the necessity
of leaving London.

" I cannot subsist much longer," she says ; " it is
time to retire. I write this in such haste that I hardly
know what I say, having a thousand things to do, with
little help and little heart. I feel that I am very unfit
for the business of this world." . . . . . And she adds
soon after, " The Chancellor earnestly assures me of

his friendship, and I think he intends to do what he can for me with the King, so that I have every reason to hope the best. I resign myself to the will of God."

In spite of her unfitness for mundane affairs, Lady Derby had not forgotten to write thus to her sister-in-law on the 31st of October, while speaking of the envoys sent by Charles II. to congratulate Louis XIV. on the birth of his son :—

"They have with them Mr. Hyde, a younger son of the Chancellor, who is a great favourite with their Royal Highnesses; I write to your son to beg that he will make known to him how much I respect his father and mother. I am sure he will not refuse to grant me this favour, and that you, dear sister, will not fail to remind him of it."

She wrote from Knowsley on the 24th of January, 1662, very much interested in a preacher, who had just come from France :—

"The King says that M. Morus is the finest preacher he has ever heard; I know that he is a great friend of yours, as M. Duret is of mine, and one that I highly esteem. M. Morus lodges at Somerset" (House or Street ?) "I believe the French Church is strongly opposed to him, but that has not prevented his preaching before the King, and their Royal Highnesses, at St James's, which he did on Sunday the 12th of this

month, with great success. I own that I am very
much disappointed at not being able to hear him, and
regret exceedingly my change from London; but I
assure you that nothing but extreme necessity would
have driven me away."

And again on the 1st of April :—

"We are very much surprised at the news you
have sent of Madame's accouchement; she is young
enough to have many sons and daughters, if she goes
on as she has begun. I am astonished that the Queen,
her mother, had not made all the necessary preparations. Mademoiselle, then, has lost her title. . . . .

"The King has again sent me his promise, by
Lady Ormond, and I am assured that I need have no
further doubt as to this matter, in which I resign
myself to the will of God. It is my sole desire to be
able to serve Him, and to forward the fortunes of my
younger children, for both they and I are in a sad condition. It was pure necessity that drove me from
London, which is certainly a fine place ; and, above all
other reasons, I regret it on account of M. Morus. If
God should ever give me the means of returning there,
I will do my utmost to be of service to him. Besides
what I should wish to do out of friendship to you, I
own that I have an extreme desire to hear him preach.
They say that Prince Rupert is going to live in Eng-

land ; no doubt he will find it to his advantage, for he is very much liked. I wish him a good and virtuous wife, and one who is known to you."

At Thouars, and at the Hotel de la Trémoille, great preparations were being made for the marriage of the only daughter of the house. She was no longer young ; she must have been at least thirty ; her mother and her aunt had carefully examined the pretensions of a great number of suitors, but their offers had all been refused by her ; this time, however, she said yes. On the 3rd of June, 1662, Lady Derby wrote :—

" My youngest son met M. Morus on the day that the King gave his assent to the Bills in Parliament, and from him he heard of the marriage of Mademoiselle your daughter. I wrote to him to beg that he would send me the particulars, but to my great regret he was gone when my letter arrived. I know this Prince by name only " (Bernard de Saxe Weimar, Duc de Jéna), " but you may believe, dear sister, how much pleased I am to hear of it, and that I wish your daughter as much happiness and contentment as if she were my own. Do me the honour, dear sister, to send me the particulars by M. de Rosemont,* for I am

---

* The Duc de la Trémoille's man of business, to whom Lady Derby wrote with this curious address :—" Monsieur, Monsieur de Rosemont, Logé chez le Sr Froisart, couturier en la Place du Pont St. Michel, vis-a-vis de Samourier, patissier, à Paris."

extremely anxious to hear them. I know well that
the marriage of an only daughter must have overwhelmed you with business, and I cannot expect you to
write. May God give you as much happiness as with
all my heart I pray you may have. When I know that
the marriage is over, I will not fail to write to you more
fully. You have heard, no doubt, about the King's
marriage, and how much pleased he is with the Queen
his wife, to whom my daughters went to pay their
respects yesterday; they think her Majesty is very
agreeable. The King is very much in love with her;
but her women are not liked. The husband of one of
them entreated the King not to kiss his wife when he
saluted her, which they say he very willingly promised
as she is not at all pretty. The Queen, I believe
liked her journey very much, having never before been
in a carriage, but only in a litter. She was a whole
month at sea, and was very ill. She has never worn
anything on her head either at night or in the day, a
custom which she still continues. They say she is
very strict in her religion, and she is to have priests
and other subjects of the King about her, which will
make her more so. May God preserve to us our
religion. I am positively assured that the King will do
me the honour to keep his promise to me; it is known
to everybody, and if Monsieur your brother would

interest the Duke of St. Albans * in my favour, the Queen, his mistress, would not oppose it. All people of consequence tell me that I may count upon it, and if it were not for the hope of being able to serve God I should not wish for it so much. I hope also, through God's grace, that I may be enabled to serve their Majesties by the care and fidelity with which I should devote myself to them. M. Morus, I hear, is certainly coming back ; he stands very well, they say, with the Duke of St. Albans. If I get this appointment, I hope to be of service to him."

Lady Derby wrote again on the 3rd of October, on the subject of a horse which she was commissioned to buy for the Duchesse de la Trémoille, adding :—

"At our Court nothing is spoken of but amusements, in which our Queen takes little pleasure. The Queen, her mother-in-law, was never gayer or more happy. Do me the honour to let me hear if Madame, your daughter, has left you, and how she has been received at her new home. I pray to God for her happiness."

Lady Derby's next letter is written from Brierton, on the 25th of November .—

"Your letters of the 23rd and 26th reached me at

* Formerly Lord Jermyn, a favourite of Queen Henrietta Maria.

a place a day's journey from Knowsley, the house of a
good friend of mine, a daughter of the Earl of Norwich,
—better known to you by his name of Goring. I
think I was wrong to leave London against my own
feeling and that of all my friends, at a time, too, when
I might have improved my affairs; but I was forced
to it by absolute necessity, not having enough to
support me, and being in continual misery about the
payment of my debts. All sorts of people refused to
supply me with the most necessary things. What
troubles me most is the thought that I might be of
use to you if I were there. When I took leave of his
Majesty he repeated the promise which I told you of
before. The Chancellor, though very ill of the gout,
gives me many assurances of his friendship, and has
promised to speak to the King for me that my pension
may be secured for several years, which would enable
me to make arrangements for the payment of my
debts, for which I am very much pressed. I hear
from one who is a good judge that this will be done.
I am sure you must have heard that the Parliament
has begun to sit again, and that the King's speech
gave great satisfaction to his people and faithful
subjects. We all hope he will remember those who
have always been loyal to him and his father. His
Highness the Duke of York has returned from Dun-

kirk.* There are still many conspiracies, and some very strange letters have been found in the possession of a Presbyterian minister. May God preserve his Majesty. I told the Prime Minister what you informed me; he answered, that they had had the same intelligence before. I am infinitely obliged to your son for the care that he promises to take of Mr. Hyde. I do not understand how M. de la Tour can say that I did not tell him you had written to me in his favour : I assured him that I would do all I could to serve him. I think he was displeased because I have not placed a little French boy in the service of my daughter Dorchester : her husband does not wish her to have a page, for he does not like French customs."

Lady Derby hoped in vain, for, though the Chancellor was favourable, and the King had given his promise to make her governess to his children, these children still remained unborn. Soon after, the violence of popular feeling obliged the Chancellor Clarendon to leave England. When the Countess next wrote from Knowsley, on the 6th of February, 1663, she was recovering from an illness :—

" If the winter is as severe with you as it is here, it

---

* Charles II. had just sold Dunkirk to Louis XIV. for four hundred thousand pounds.

is wonderful how your health can improve. I have
been very much indisposed for more than a month;
but God has been pleased to restore my health, and I
hope He will give me grace to employ it better than
I have hitherto done. My illness prevented me from
telling you that his Royal Highness has been pleased
to appoint your nephew Stanley to be his first and sole
gentleman of the bed-chamber, which is a great thing
for him ; and, what is of more consequence still, the
honour was conferred upon him without any solicita-
tion by his Royal Highness, to whom and to the
Duchess he is alone indebted.

"His younger brother has obtained a cornetcy in
the King's Guards ; his Majesty did him the honour of
assuring him that this was only a beginning ; and I
hope it may be so. . . . . I have only to add my
prayers that God may grant you many happy years,
with every blessing you can desire. Permit me to
say the same to Monsieur my brother."

Here ends the correspondence of Charlotte de la
Trémoille, Countess of Derby, with her sister-in-law,
Marie de la Tour d'Auvergne, Duchesse de la Tré-
moille. From this time till her death, which took
place at Knowsley, on the 31st of March, 1664, Lady
Derby wrote no more.

We have no details of her last moments ; we know

not even if her children were with her, or if her sister-
in-law, who did not long survive her, knew of her illness. Of the death of the Countess Charlotte no other
record remains, except the Latin words inscribed by
the clergyman at Knowsley in the parish register of
burials, after the names and titles of the deceased,
" *Post funera virtus.*"

Such an epitaph might well be written over Charlotte de la Trémoille. At once haughty and humble,
her character bore no resemblance to the portrait that
Sir Walter Scott has drawn of her in his *Peveril of the
Peak*. It was unjust to attribute to her the fate which,
after the Restoration, befell Captain William Christian.
He was found guilty of insurrection and of treason,
for having surrendered to the Parliamentary Commissioners the Isle of Man, together with the widow and
children of the Earl of Derby, his liege lord. But it
was Lord Derby's successor, that son so long estranged
from his parents on account of his marriage, and ever
after regarded coldly by his mother, although forgiven
by his father,—it was Charles, Lord Strange, afterwards eighth Earl of Derby, who, in January, 1662,
out of respect to his father's memory, caused William
Christian to be shot. This was done by virtue of a
local sentence, which, in August, 1663, was declared
illegal by the Privy Council of Charles II., as contrary

to the Act of Indemnity. Lord Derby maintained that he had proceeded according to the laws of the Isle of Man, which was a separate and independent kingdom ; but he was not in favour at Court, and his arguments were held to be invalid. Not only was his right to the exercise of sovereign justice denied, but the King's ill will went so far that he refused to sanction a Bill which had been passed by both Houses of Parliament for restoring to the family the estates of James, Earl of Derby, confiscated in 1651, on the re-payment by his son of the inconsiderable sums which had been given for them.

Long afterwards, at the commencement of the eighteenth century, James, tenth Earl of Derby, who had succeeded to the title on the death of his brother William without heirs male, and who spent the last years of his life in retirement at Knowsley, devoted his leisure to the rebuilding of the house, over the entrance of which he caused the following inscription to be engraved :—

" This was erected by James, Earl of Derby, Lord of Man and the Isles, grandson of James, Earl of Derby, by Charlotte, daughter of Claude, Duke of Trémoille, who was beheaded at Bolton, October 15th, 1651, for strenuously adhering to Charles II., who refused a Bill unanimously passed by both Houses of

Parliament, for restoring to the family the estates which he had lost by his loyalty to him."

In spite of the brilliant proofs of passionate devotion which she had given to her husband, Charlotte de la Trémoille seems during her latter years not to have shared in her son's hereditary hatred and revenge. Heroic by nature, she sought no opportunities of displaying her heroism, nor was she ambitious of critical positions or important adventures,—yet none of these could have been found—none ever were found—to which her high heart and firm will were not equal, and that spontaneously, without either effort or premeditation.

Endowed with the noblest qualities of her era, of her race, and of her station, resolute to perform all duties, ready for all sacrifices, capable of any heroism, but too proud to make a merit of these things, she accepted, from a sense of honour as much as from conscientiousness, the trials of her destiny. Pious by education as well as by conviction, she nevertheless lacked that deep and stedfast fervour which was a distinguishing feature of French Protestantism in the age which preceded her own. Her piety, though earnest and sincere, did not occupy itself with minute subtleties; she was simple in her faith as in her heroism, and no more thought of troubling herself with scruples than she would have hesitated to accept the fate of a martyr, if her conscience or her honour had required it. After having borne so noble a part in the struggles and sufferings of a great revolution, when these stern times were succeeded by a reign of less severity, and the Restoration of Charles II. revived in England the manners and magnificence of a Court that soon became as profligate as it was frivolous, Charlotte de la Trémoille, with an ease and elasticity of nature, characteristic rather of France, her native country, than of England, the land of her adoption, looked on at these things without anger. Untouched by either the frivolity or the corruption of the Court, or, perhaps, not recognising sufficiently its evils and dangers, she played the part of a Court lady as naturally as in the time of the Civil War she had done that of a heroine.

Living in a foreign country and in the midst of foreign manners which she frankly adopted, called upon to endure, and enduring nobly, the most unexpected trials, she nevertheless retained something of the prejudices, habits, and tastes of her own country, and of the rank in which she was born. She was pre-eminently a "grande dame" and a noble lady; frank and resolute, loyal and faithful; a woman of whom the great houses from which she was sprung and to which she was allied might well be proud,—one who was worthy to bear upon her arms the two mottoes which had governed her life :—" Je maintiendrai," and " Sans changer." *

* The mottoes of William the Silent, Prince of Orange, and of the Earls of Derby.

THE END.